CONTENTS

PAPER DOLLS

Jeanine Joyner

First Printing 2019

ISBN 9781705862353

Jeanine Joyner
alifeofsimplejoys@gmail.com
alifeofsimplejoys.com

For Hadassah.

Your light grows brighter with each passing day.

MELODY

The summer sun shone mercilessly, baking the back of her neck. Her ponytail swung in time while the dead branch in her hand—found on the edge of a neighbor's yard and now used as a walking stick—left dots in the dry North Texas dirt as she plodded along the road in her new white Keds.

The shoes were stiff, quickly rubbing a blister on her right heel. Melody stooped to adjust the bandage that she had put on in an attempt to prevent this very thing. Sighing, she continued walking, wiping sweat that ran down her temples with the back of one hand and swinging the stick like a baton with the other.

A passing car drifted away from the shoulder along which she was walking and toward the center of the road in order to give her room to meander unharmed. The mismatched trailer houses lined the road like a disassembled train, chain-link fences serving as property line markers. A dog yapped at her in short shrill bursts as she walked, oblivious to her surroundings. Ignoring the dog, she was singing a song under her breath.

Melody reached the hill at the end of Randall Road. She bent forward a little as she walked. She was tempted to turn around and go home, her heel was hurting so badly, but at last she reached the top. Her calves were burning from the steep climb. She was relieved to pass under the shade trees along the right and get reprieve from the brutal sun.

Almost there.

She adjusted the bandage again, surprised at how quickly the large blister had formed. How stupid to wear her new shoes on this long walk! She was limping now.

Dumb, dumb, dumb.

Finally the small green sign was within view: Wall Street. She made the right turn and picked up the pace when Kelley's avocado green family trailer neared on the left. Scraggly grass and dandelions had completely overtaken the long-neglected flower beds. The trailers lining this block were very different from the modest brick house Melody and her family lived in on New Hope Lane. They appeared to be barely standing atop the makeshift foundations on which they had been set years ago. Rickety. Melody took off the offending shoe before going up the rusty metal steps and knocking on the door. Scuffling sounds came from inside, and the weathered brass handle turned with a squeak. Mrs. Collins stood at the door, a cigarette dangling from her mouth.

"Kelley!" she yelled over her shoulder, "Mel's here!" Then, turning her face back to Melody, she smiled through the smoke coming out of her nostrils. "Hi Mel. Come on in."

Melody stepped past Mrs. Collins into the hazy darkness of the dimly-lit trailer. Kelly came bouncing into the room, grinning.

"Hey."

"Hey," said Melody.

"Wanna go over to Granny's?"

"Sure."

Kelley took Melody by the arm and the two quickly darted out into the fresh air, down the steps, and across the lawn to the rusty white trailer where Kelley's beloved Grandma Violet and Papa Joe lived. Melody couldn't help but smile as they ran into their house without knocking. There were never formalities needed around Granny V. She lived life with an open door policy to anyone who was willing to take the time to visit her. There were many things Violet loved, and her grandbabies were at the very top of the list.

"Hi girls," said Violet from the refrigerator. She appeared to be at a loss as to why she was standing there. "Oh!" she said, and reached in for a can of Dr. Pepper. She popped the top and turned toward Melody and Kelley. "What're you up to?"

The girls shrugged in unison. "Just hanging out."

Violet adjusted her housecoat over her thin frame and walked across to the small living room where she sat on the faded brown sofa, leaving room on both sides for the girls. They eagerly flanked her on the couch, knowing she would keep them entertained. Papa Joe smiled from his usual spot in the thread-bare tweed recliner positioned across the room near the window as he rustled his newspaper and turned the page.

"Well," said Violet. "Any news? Gossip? Juicy tidbits?"

The girls grinned. Kelley spoke first.

"School starts in two weeks."

Melody chimed in, "And I'm so bored I'm actually ready for it. Mom has been working every day, and Dad is so busy at the shop that we barely see him. Jake and I have resorted to watching Sesame Street twice this week."

Violet laughed. It was a deep, raspy laugh resulting from years of smoking. "Sounds like you need to spend more time over here, Mel!"

Kelley nodded in agreement. "Jimmy and Caleb are about to drive me crazy. You know I'd rather hang out with you and Granny V than my brothers.. I could have been so happy as an

3

only child." She sighed. "Mom doesn't even pay attention to their fighting any more. She just stares out the kitchen window and yells for Kristy or me to keep the baby out of their way."

Violet patted Kelley's knee. "Well, your mama has a lot on her plate, honey. She is doing the best she can."

"I know," Kelley said softly.

"Well!" Violet jumped up as if the conversation was starting completely over. Which, actually, it was. "Y'all hungry?" She danced across the room, back to the kitchen, and reached for the radio perched on the windowsill above the sink. Music came pouring into the room as she opened the pantry door. She reached in and her hand emerged with a bag of M&M's, and the girls immediately bounded over to join her. Popping the tiny chocolates in their mouths, they giggled as a popular beat echoed off the dingy windows while they all danced and bobbed their heads to the song, including Violet. She enjoyed the modern songs as much as the youngsters, and for that they loved her even more.

Spinning and shaking, they danced and sang at the top of their lungs, not caring that the song was a bit inappropriate for twelve-year-olds. It was fun. It was catchy. And the singer was really, really cute.

The afternoon flew by. They talked and sang and talked some more and, before she knew it, the time came for Melody to walk home.

In her new Keds.

Which she now hated.

She hugged Grandma Violet and squeezed her best friend's arm as she left the trailer, shoes in hand. If she was careful to pick smooth pavement or soft grass along the way, surely her feet would survive the walk home.

CHANGE

"**I**'m home!"

The screen door slammed behind her as Melody walked into her house. Her mother came out of the bedroom, barefoot but still in her work clothes. She was a secretary at a local church and wore heels on most days, which she kicked off with great pleasure once she was home. She floated across the room and wrapped Melody in her signature bear hug.

"Hey babe," she said into her daughter's hair. "I missed you. Where've you been?"

"At Kelley's," Melody said, relaxing into her mother's embrace. She loved the comforting familiarity of her mother's hugs.

Allie took a step back from her daughter and smiled, then frowned.

"Why aren't you wearing shoes?"

Melody sheepishly pulled her left hand from behind her back with the shoes dangling from her fingertips. "They gave me bad blisters."

"You know better than to wear new shoes like that until they have been broken in. Walking home barefoot is dangerous. You could have gotten glass or something worse in your foot."

"I know, Mom. But I didn't. It's okay. I just wanted to show the shoes to Kelley. It was stupid, and now my feet hurt."

"Well, come in here and clean up. I am about to start dinner. You can take a bath while I'm cooking, and soak your feet. I've got more Band-Aids in the kitchen, and I'll put some salve on the blisters when you are finished with your bath."

"Okay."

Melody went into her room and dug through her top dresser drawer for some underwear. Grabbing a t-shirt off the back of her desk chair and a pair of shorts off the floor, she went into the bathroom that she shared with her younger brother Jake. She turned on the faucet and put her hand under the gushing water to test the temperature. When it was warm enough, she plugged the bathtub and waited for it to fill. She checked the blister on her right heel and grimaced. It had popped and looked disgusting, weeping clear fluid, and the skin that once protected it dangled and had become discolored. Sigh. Her left foot was in better condition. It had a blister as well, but at least this one was still intact, providing some protection for the tender flesh beneath. Both feet, though, were filthy from the long walk home.

As the bathtub filled, Melody stripped off her sweaty tank top and shorts. She climbed into the warm water, and her feet immediately thanked her as the throbbing subsided. She sat in silence, listening to the water lapping the edges of the tub and the occasional drip from the faucet. Smells were beginning to drift in from the kitchen where her mother was humming as she cooked.

Burgers. Yum.

Melody heard the front door open and smiled. Dad was home. The door shut behind him with a bang, and his deep voice boomed a greeting to her mom and Jake. She heard him exclaim when her mother told him she was making hamburgers, "Mm-mm! Now that sounds good!"

Melody got out of the bathtub and dried herself off with a pink towel from the hook on the back of the door. She put on her clean clothes, leaving the dirty ones piled on the floor next to the bathtub, and ran down the hall, hair still dripping, to greet her father, who was leaning against the counter beside the stove with his ankles crossed, popping pickles in his mouth as he listened to Allie's description of her day.

"Daddy!" she cried happily.

"Hey birdie!" he said as he met her halfway and engulfed her in his big arms. He smelled of machine oil and aftershave. Melody turned her head to avoid the scratchiness of his beard on her face and wrapped her thin arms as far as she could around his big frame. How she loved her father.

"Melody spent the afternoon at Granny V's," said her mom. "Look at her feet—she tore them up wearing new shoes and no socks."

"Ouch, honey. That looks painful," said Pete as Melody turned to give him a glimpse of her raw heels. Melody shrugged and followed her mom into the kitchen for salve and fresh bandages.

"What was Violet up to?" asked Pete as Allie searched the medicine box for the tube of antibiotic ointment. Melody sat on the countertop near the sink, swinging her legs as she waited.

"Aw, nothing much. Kelley and I just hung out and listened to music. She gave us M&M's, too."

"Hmm," said Pete. "She seems to love having you girls around."

"Yeah, she is lots of fun. And she's so nice. We can talk about anything and she never acts like what we say is dumb or weird. She just listens and seems to 'get it,'" said Melody.

Pete and Allie exchanged glances over Melody's head as Allie rubbed the ointment on Melody's blisters. What a blessing, at this age, for their daughter to have someone in her life like Violet. Even though she might give similar advice as they would, Melody was much more likely to take it to heart when it was coming from someone other than her parents. Violet possessed a wealth of wisdom, but it didn't seem to show up in an out-of-date sort of way. Her wisdom was quiet, understated even. She knew when to interject a word at just the right time and then let it rest. Like a seed on fertile soil, it would take root at the right time. She knew kids very well, especially girls, and had the gift of subtle teaching strategically embedded in a nice, big dose of humor.

"How does that feel?" asked Allie as she placed the second bandage on Melody's heels.

"Good. Thanks, Mom." Melody jumped down from the countertop and looked at the hamburger patties sizzling in the cast-iron skillet on the stove. "Dinner smells good. Do you need help?"

"Actually I am just about finished. I just need to tear some lettuce and slice a tomato. Want to get the ketchup out of the fridge? And there is a bag of chips over there by the can opener. We can have those with the burgers if you want." Allie cupped her hands around her mouth, speaking loudly into the open room. "Jake! Time to eat!"

Jake came stumbling out of his bedroom, a model airplane in one hand, and—what was that, a superglue container?—stuck to the other. He was shaking his hand furiously and appeared almost panicked.

"Mom! I can't get this off!" Pete and Allie burst into laughter while Melody fought embarrassment at her brother's near-tearful state. He could be a bit ... dramatic. While holding a wing on his model airplane he had apparently held the glue tube in the other, not realizing the glue had run down the side and was securing the tube and his index finger firmly together. "Mom, seriously! It hurts! Help me!"

"Hang on a second, Jake. Calm down. I can get it off if you will let me." Allie sent Melody to get a bottle of nail polish remover from the bathroom while she examined Jake's finger. Melody returned quickly, stifling laughter at her brother's wild shaking of his hand. Allie worked efficiently, easing the glue away from Jake's skin until, at last, his hand was free. "Now go wash that smell off your hands and come eat before everyone's burgers get cold."

Pete was already building his hamburger. It had been a long and busy afternoon since he had eaten lunch, and his growling stomach was not going to wait a minute longer. He sat at the head of the table and popped a potato chip in his mouth, then another. One by one the rest of the family joined him.

"Let's pray," he said. The four of them held hands around the small table as Pete took a deep breath and exhaled: "Father, thank you for this day. Thank you for this food. Thank you for Allie and our children. Bless us, and let us be useful to you. In Jesus' name, Amen."

"Amen," they all responded, and the room fell silent as they all dug in to their burgers.

As Pete, Allie, Melody, and Jake took their dirty dishes into the kitchen after the meal, Pete looked out the window.

"Did you notice the house across the street has sold?"

"No," said Allie. She moved closer to her husband so she could see the realtor's sign in the neighbors' yard. Hanging from two metal rings was a smaller sign that said "SOLD." "Well, it sure has. I can't help but feel sad that the DeLeons are moving. I know this is a good move for them, with Joel's promotion and all, but I sure do like Sofia. It is going to be hard to get used to not seeing her smiling face in her flower garden every morning when I drive to work. She is just so sweet."

"I'm sure the new neighbors will be nice."

"I'm sure," Allie echoed.

"We'll have to make a point to have them over once they get settled in. Maybe they will have kids! That would be great for Mel and Jake to have friends on this street."

Melody was listening to her parents' conversation as she left the kitchen and picked up a book from the stack on the coffee table before plopping down in her father's recliner. Jake was back in his room, hopefully not gluing his lips together. Then again, maybe that wouldn't be so bad. Melody giggled at her own unspoken joke.

It would be nice to have a girl on their street. As much as she loved Kelley, it was an awfully long walk to her house, and wouldn't it be fun to just look out the window, see a friendly face, and meet up on the spur of the moment?

Then again, what if the girl was mean?

Nasty?

Hateful?

Melody laughed again. She could just imagine a hate-fest, spying on the enemy across the street and journaling her every sinister move:

> *2:00 p.m.: New girl is home. She just turned on her bedroom light.*

> *2:23 p.m.: She just walked outside to check the mail. She is so ugly.*

Oh, the drama! Despite her vivid imagination, though, Melody did hope for a new friend.

A girl can never have too many of those, right?

SHOPPING

Shopping for school clothes was one of Melody's favorite traditions with her mom. With less than two weeks remaining in this summer break, she was ready to pick out her new look for the year. Her mother had been watching the newspaper and television ads and was waiting until just the right moment, just the right sale, just the right bargain. Melody was afraid if they waited much longer she would be going to school in last year's too-small jeans, skirts, and tops, but at last her mom informed her that she was taking this Tuesday afternoon off and they were going shopping.

Melody lay on the sofa, waiting not-so-patiently for her mother's lunchtime arrival. She was dressed and trying to concentrate on her book while keeping one eye on the front door, when her mom came flying in, all smiles, and flung off her high heels. They landed askew next to the bookcase, and she sang out, "Time to go!"

"Yay!" said Melody, closing her book and springing up off the sofa in excitement. The book would have to wait!

"Great," mumbled Jake. He wasn't quite as enthusiastic as his mom and sister. He didn't mind new clothes, but shopping with the girls could mean hours of trying things on, deciding what goes with what, and excruciatingly-painful discussions of patterns, colors, and whatnot. If he had things his way, he'd walk into the nearest clothing store, buy a handful of jeans and t-shirts, and walk out. Bam. Ten minutes from start to finish, and he could get back to his beloved model airplanes. But no. He had to go shopping. He only hoped he would score some ice cream for all his trouble and patience. And maybe a new model to build.

Allie told the kids to give her just a minute to change clothes. She walked into her bedroom and came out moments later in jeans, a blue polo-style shirt, and her well-worn tennis shoes. Her shoulder-length hair was pulled back in a ponytail. She picked up her purse from the table in the entry hall where she had laid it and motioned for the kids to follow her out the door, which they did.

Outside, the skies were slightly overcast—a welcome relief in August. The heat had been oppressive for weeks, with temperatures over 100 degrees and no rain in sight. The grass had turned brown, the trees looked tired, and the farmers were complaining. Cottony white clouds crawled across the expanse above the trees, accented by the occasional dark cloud that made the residents of Parkland dare to hope for rain. Allie and the kids got into the car, a gently-used burgundy Ford mini-van with a small dent in the driver's side door where it had been dinged by a careless neighboring car in the church parking lot. Melody and Jake buckled their seat belts while their mom started the car and began backing out of the driveway.

"I wonder who is going to move in to that house," said Jake, his eyes on the sign in the yard across the street as his mother shifted the car out of reverse into first gear.

"I don't know," said Allie, "but I hope they take as good care of that yard as Sofia has. I have loved the view of her flowers every year. She is such a gifted gardener."

"Much better than anyone else on the street, huh?" remarked

Melody. "I mean, look at Betty Barber's house. It's like a desert in her yard. Barely even any grass growing."

"Well, Betty is old, Mel. She can barely walk without help, and I doubt she has the energy to pull weeds or water her yard."

"Yeah, but she has the energy to yell at us when we walk by and weird us out!" said Jake. "She's creepy."

"Jake," said Allie disapprovingly, "she is not creepy; she's lonely. You need to be nice to her. She loves kids."

"For breakfast," mumbled Jake under his breath, thinking his mother could not hear. Of course she had heard him. She also understood that further conversation about his disrespect of Betty Barber would get her nowhere, so she dropped the subject.

The drive to the department store was about twenty minutes long. The radio provided entertainment while the kids chattered—and bickered—back and forth. Melody talked about the clothes she wanted while Jake gave his not-so-humble opinion on her taste in fashion. She ignored him as long as she could before punching him in the shoulder.

"Ow!" he yelled. "Mom, she's hitting me!"

"Stop, now, you two. We are almost there." Jake glared at Melody and she stuck out her tongue at him. He angrily crossed his arms and looked out the window as they neared their destination.

Allie steered the vehicle into the parking lot of Balyard's department store. Its three stories soared above them as they got out and walked across the pavement to the entrance where a large, yellow vinyl sign advertised the big sale:

Back to School Bash!

50 percent off all school staples!

Deep discounts on red-line clearance items!

The store buzzed with activity as families sorted through racks laden with tops, pants, and accessories for their children. It was a happy busy. Melody immediately headed past the cosmetics counters toward the Juniors' department, walking so quickly that Allie had to grab Jake by the hand and almost drag him along to keep up with her. He stood, hands in the pockets of his denim shorts, scowling while Melody squealed with delight at the selection of clothing.

"Look, Mom! I saw this dress on TV the other day! Isn't it cute? Oh, look at this one! I wonder if it's too short for school?"

Blah, blah, blah . . . Jake sighed in boredom and looked around. Just two aisles over was the boys' clothing. So close, but yet so far. He hoped Melody could make a decision quickly, but he knew better. She and their mom already had several outfits draped over their arms.

"Jake, she needs to try these on. Come over here with us to the dressing room," said Allie.

Jake followed reluctantly and, at his mother's suggestion, sank down into one of the plush chairs positioned just outside the ladies' dressing room. His mom and sister disappeared behind the swinging door, and he could hear them talking as Melody tried on clothes. He leaned his head back and closed his eyes, daydreaming about the latest launch of the space shuttle and just how utterly cool it would be to fly that thing, when he heard a cry.

His eyes flew open and locked immediately with the frightened eyes of a pale little girl, about five years old, staring at him from behind a rack of frilly formal dresses, the kind usually worn in beauty pageants. Her big blue eyes blinked twice, then she looked away. A woman was with her, telling her sternly that she was going to try on the dresses she had draped over her left arm. The little girl nervously pulled at a blonde curl that fell

14

over her shoulder and said, "But they are scratchy, mama. They make me itch."

The woman bent closer to the little girl and said something back, too low in volume for Jake to make out, but the little girl immediately ducked her head and nodded. The two went through the swinging doors into the dressing rooms, walking quickly past Jake, who couldn't understand why there was so suddenly much tension in the room.

At last his mom and sister reappeared. Melody happily held up two dresses and smiled. "I'm getting these, and those," she said, pointing to the jeans and shirts her mother held.

"Great. Awesome. My turn now?" said Jake impatiently.

"Sure, let's go see what they have for you," said Allie. The three of them walked over to the boys' clothing section, and Jake, true to form, selected his school wardrobe with the sweep of a hand.

"Jeans and t-shirts, mom. That's all I want."

"Well, that's fine, but you still need to try them on for size. You have grown over the summer, you know." Jake sighed and dutifully followed his mom to the boys' dressing room where he tried on two styles of jeans and a couple of shirts just to be sure they fit. Satisfied, his mother selected a few more to complete his fall wardrobe, and they all headed to the front of the store to pay.

Jake couldn't shake the odd feeling, though, that something was strange about that little girl and the lady she called mama. Why did she look afraid? She was just trying on clothes, and from what he could see she was being decked out in very fancy ones. Obviously they weren't school clothes, so maybe she was in pageants or something? He didn't know, but he hoped the little girl had been able to find what she wanted . . . and that he was wrong about the feeling that she was afraid. Maybe she just really hated dressing up.

HARD NEWS

Smoke curled gracefully from Violet's cigarette as her granddaughter and Melody sat across from one another at the checkerboard on the floor of her cluttered living room. She noticed the brown shag carpet could use a good vacuuming, but the girls didn't seem to mind. The television muttered under its breath about the Space Shuttle Discovery's current mission. Beautiful NASA photographs of the Earth from space filled the screen.

"I stink at this game," complained Kelley as Melody took out another of her black checker pieces.

Violet laughed. "Well, I'm afraid you come by your poor strategic planning skills naturally my dear. I love to play games, but I am not good at winning. It's just fun to spend time with you two." She smiled at the girls, her cheeks pulling back into deep wrinkles and her eyes almost disappearing.

"Yesssss," breathed Melody as she made another move. She was not exactly a gracious winner.

"Aw, Mel, come on," said Kelley as Melody trapped her once again.

"Sorry, Kel. I can't help it! You wouldn't want me to let

you win, would you?" Melody tried unsuccessfully to stifle her smile.

"Oh, please. Like I could win. Hmph." Kelley sat back and turned her attention to the TV. "Who is that?"

They all looked up then. On the screen was a man being led out of a courthouse in handcuffs. Violet walked across the room and turned up the volume before returning to the sofa, this time lowering herself until she was sitting cross-legged on the floor with her back against the sofa's seat cushions.

"*. . . Richards will spend twenty years behind bars for his crimes. The family of the victim is not speaking out at this time, but we can only imagine their relief at knowing this dangerous man will no longer walk the streets of Lawton.*"

The five o'clock news anchorwoman shook her head as she took a breath, reading the stack of papers in front of her and changing the subject to something . . . lighter—a local car wash raising funds for the high school band's trip to Austin for the state marching contest.

Kelley looked at her grandmother. "What did that guy do, Granny V?"

"From what I heard yesterday, he kidnapped a young girl and had her tied up somewhere. She was found alive, but very sick. I don't know the details and, honestly, I wouldn't tell you if I did. Like Corrie Ten Boom says, some things are too heavy for children to carry."

"Huh?" said both girls. "Who is she?"

"Ah, Corrie Ten Boom was a wonderful woman," said Violet softly. "She was imprisoned many years ago during the Jewish Holocaust and lived to tell about it. Once she asked her father to explain something that he felt was too mature of a subject to discuss with her. He responded by telling her to pick up the suitcase he had set on the ground. Of course, it was too heavy for her.

Then he said that some of her questions were like that suitcase —that she needed to let her father carry them for her until she was old enough to carry the weight herself."

Violet sat back, leaning against the sofa behind her. "Unfortunately, there are a lot of bad things that happen in the world. You girls only get to be young and innocent once. I don't want to spoil that. No way. There are a lot of things you don't need to worry about until you are older."

Melody and Kelley looked at each other and smiled. They loved Violet. They trusted her. It felt good to be sheltered even though, in their pre-teen minds, they were practically adults.

"Want some M&M's?" asked Violet, unfolding herself from her sitting position on the floor with the help of the sofa, and changing the mood of the room.

"You know it!" said Kelley. The girls jumped up and followed her to the cookie jar. They each got a handful of chocolates and walked outside to sit on the top step leading up to the door of Violet's trailer.

The sun was hot, beating down on the weathered wood. Across the lawn, three children ran around in bathing suits, squealing as they darted in and out of the water spraying from a lawn sprinkler that slowly fanned back and forth, back and forth.

"I can't believe school starts next week," said Kelley.

"Are you excited?" asked Violet.

"Well, I guess so. But it stinks to be going back in the same old clothes I wore last year. Mama said we can't afford to go shopping. Shoot, we can barely afford food any more. If it wasn't for the free stuff we get from the food bank, we'd probably starve. Mama tries to hide that she's sad, but I can tell. Sometimes her eyes are red in the mornings..." Kelley's voice trailed off.

It had been eighteen months since her father had disappeared. His absence was devastating. If he had died, at least the family would have received life insurance money. But as far as they knew he was alive and well—and living with another woman. He had met her at the factory where he had worked all of Kelley's life. There had been no warning that he was leaving. He just told Nora one day that he was tired of all the baggage and wanted to start over—start fresh— without her.

Without their family.

Kelley's mother had suddenly seen all the puzzle pieces come together—strange behaviors and unexplained "wrong numbers" when their phone rang and she answered. Looking back was painfully 20/20, but by the time she realized what was happening it was too late, and she was left to raise their five children alone.

"I'm sorry, honey," said Violet. "I wish I had the money to help you buy clothes. I really do."

"I know, Granny."

Melody was quiet, embarrassed at her shopping spree earlier that week. Of course, her family wasn't wealthy by any stretch of the imagination, but she always had what she needed. She had to wait until it went on clearance, of course. Her parents were very careful, accounting for every dollar in their paychecks and giving generously to their church even when money was tight.

Suddenly, Melody had an idea.

"Kel, would you want to look through my clothes and see what you can wear? I have stuff that is a little too small for me and maybe it would fit you . . . I don't know. It's not brand new, but at least it would be something."

Kelley smiled ruefully. "Thanks, Mel. I don't know . . . it is one thing to borrow your stuff because we are friends, but I don't want to become a charity case."

Melody frowned and reached out to touch Kelley's shoulder.

"You're not. Not at all. But we would just give it to Goodwill—might as well give it to you."

"I'll think about it," said Kelley, battling her pride. "Maybe next time I come over I'll look at your stuff."

"Okay, any time," said Melody, not wanting to make Kelley feel any more uncomfortable than she already did.

"You are a good friend, Mel," said Violet. "No wonder Kelley loves you so much. She is blessed to have you, you know." Melody looked away as Granny V praised her, feeling uneasy. Violet lit another cigarette, holding it midair for a while and watching the smoke rise.

The kids across the lawn screamed in delight, their wet bodies glistening in the late afternoon sun. The grass at their feet was quickly becoming a mud pit, and their legs were splattered with the reddish-brown muck. They didn't care. Life was idyllic in that moment. No worries.

Just as childhood should be.

MOVING DAY

The countdown to the first day of school was almost over. It was Monday afternoon. Today was Labor Day and tomorrow school bells would be ringing once again. Melody sat on her bed, cross-legged, with an open book in her lap. She stared off into space, daydreaming about nothing, when she heard the loud hiss of air brakes outside in the street. She jumped up and ran over to her window, pushing aside the blue curtains.

The new neighbors!

Excitedly, she watched as workmen unloaded furniture: couches, beds, dressers, tables, and countless boxes. Melody hoped for signs of kids, and grinned when she saw a white, wrought iron, twin-sized headboard, a pink crib, and a dollhouse emerge from the moving truck.

Yes! A family was moving in with children! And girls, no less! What fun!

She watched for a few more minutes but didn't see any signs of the neighbors themselves. Walking back over to her bed, she sat down on the edge and picked up her book. Oh, how she hoped for a friend her age.

"Melody, honey, can you come here please?" Her mother's voice was muffled, coming from another part of the house. Melody walked out of her room and down the hall.

"Where are you?"

"In here . . . in the laundry room."

Melody followed her mother's voice and found her on the attic ladder with her head in the rafters. She giggled.

"What are you doing, Mom?"

"I was going through stuff to give to Goodwill and decided to see what we had hiding up here. I have a big box to bring down but I need to pass it to you so I can get down this ladder without breaking a leg."

"Here, hand it to me. I'm ready," said Melody with her arms out, palms up. Her mother carefully balanced on the ladder, leaning against the rungs for support, while lowering a box full of picture frames and old wall art to Melody. Once it was securely handed off, Allie climbed down the last three rungs and brushed the dust off of her jeans.

"Thanks, Mel. Now, let me see." Allie looked around the small laundry room at the various bags and boxes she had collected from around the house. "That should be good. It will certainly clear out a lot of space in our closets and on our shelves! I never can understand how we manage to collect so much . . . junk."

Melody suddenly remembered her conversation with Kelley the week before. "Mom, do you think there are some things in here that we could give to Kelley?"

"Did you ever go through your clothes?"

"Yeah. But I don't know how to give them to her without making her feel bad."

Allie smiled at her daughter, glad to see her generosity and sensitivity towards her friend.

"Why don't you call her and invite her over? Then while she is here you can just 'happen' to go through all this stuff and she can take what she wants. Since we are getting rid of it anyway, it might make her feel better. In fact, whatever clothes you planned to give her should just be added in to these bags. That way it won't be so obvious and she will feel more comfortable taking the things she likes."

"Okay, that's a good idea. I can call her now?"

"Of course. We don't have anything going on the rest of the afternoon. Call her." Melody walked into the kitchen and picked up the telephone receiver, holding it to her ear while she dialed Kelley's phone number on the base, which was mounted to the wall. The phone rang three times before one of the boys answered.

"Hello?"

"Hi, who's this?"

"Jimmy. Who's this?" said Jimmy in a high, feminine voice.

"Melody, you idiot. Is Kelley there?"

"I'm really supposed to get her for you after you call me an idiot? Nice, Mel." Click.

Melody laughed. She dialed the number again and this time Mrs. Collins answered.

"Melody?"

"Yes, ma'am," she giggled. Mrs. Collins laughed softly.

"I figured that had to be you. That crazy boy. Hang on a sec, I'll get Kelley."

Moments later Kelley picked up the phone and Melody asked her if she wanted to come over.

"Oh yes, please give me a reason to bust outta here! I'll be over as soon as I can get my shoes on!"

About twenty minutes later Kelley arrived, flushed and sweaty after the long walk. Melody was sitting on the single step of their front porch in the shade of the brown awning. The moving truck across the street appeared to be almost empty.

Boy, those guys worked fast.

Melody hugged her friend and invited her to come inside. Kelley noticed the truck. "Have you met the new neighbors yet?"

"Nope, haven't even seen them. There are kids, though! I saw beds that just had to belong to a girl—maybe even a few girls!"

"Cool," said Kelley. "I hope they are nice."

"Me too." Melody led Kelley into the house and just "happened" to wander into the laundry room. "Want a Coke?"

"Yeah, that sounds good."

Melody reached up over the boxes and bags her mother had gathered where the cases of sodas were stored, taking her time to ensure that Kelley noticed the pile. It worked.

"What's all that?"

"Oh, my mom was going through stuff and plans to take all of this to Goodwill this week." She paused, not sure how to broach the subject. Kelley's eyes darted quickly away. Melody took a breath and released it. "If you want, you can look at it . . ." Her voice trailed off.

Kelley swallowed and fought with herself for a moment. She needed clothes . . . in fact she really needed clothes. Her summer growth spurt had not terribly affected her wardrobe of shorts and t-shirts. But jeans? Nothing she had finished the previous school year in fit. And, being the oldest girl in the family, she had no hand-me-downs to wear. At 5 foot 4 inches, Melody was a good three inches taller than Kelley, so anything she had outgrown would likely fit Kelley perfectly.

"Okay, I guess I can look. Thanks, Mel."

Melody breathed a sigh of relief before carefully removing the twist tie from the top of the garbage bag her mother had hastily put her old clothes in while they had waited for Kelley to walk to their house. She handed Kelley a stack of blue jeans and picked up the shirts and skirts to carry into her bedroom where Kelley could try the clothes on in privacy. They placed the stacks on her unmade bed, and Melody reached for the radio on the nightstand, pressing the power button. The station was one that played soft rock music, which Melody liked to listen to with her mother. The strains of a ballad by Lionel Ritchie filled the room.

Kelley took off her clothes and tried on a pair of acid-washed jeans and a navy blue blouse with a bold pink floral pattern across the front. The outfit was perfect. She smiled at Melody.

"These are cute! What do you think?" Kelley smoothed the shirt over her waist and let her hands rest on her thighs.

"That's perfect," said Melody. "Try this one!" She grabbed a pair of high-waisted jeans and a white sweatshirt that was designed to hang off one shoulder, with a black tank attached underneath, tossing them to Kelley, who quickly changed out of the jeans and blouse and put on the new combination.

Kelley looked at herself in the full-length mirror hanging on the back of Melody's bedroom door and turned back and forth with her hands on her hips, her heart beating happily at the thought of wearing new-to-her clothes to school and no one knowing that she didn't actually buy them. And her mom would be so relieved. Nora had apologized to Kelley over and over for their sorry financial state, hating that she could not afford to even go to Goodwill for clothes. Kelley, of course, tried her hardest to understand, but she couldn't help but battle insecurity and dread over the first day of school when all the kids would be in their brand new outfits and she would have been sporting too-short pants.

But now she could relax and look forward to the beginning of the year just like everyone else. She hugged Melody before she even realized what she was doing.

"Thank you," she whispered into Melody's hair.

"That's what friends are for, Kel. I'm glad they fit. Heck, I think they look better on you than they did on me!"

The girls giggled, enjoying the impromptu fashion show, and Lionel sang away while the moving truck pulled the metal ramp up into the trailer and backed out of the driveway across the street. In the alley behind the new neighbors' house, three girls quietly got out of a minivan with dark tinted windows and filed in to the back door of their new home, unnoticed. The youngest held the hand of the oldest, while the middle child skipped ahead, almost tripping on the threshold of the patio door as they made their way in. The van then circled the block and pulled into the driveway where a well-dressed man, woman, and toddler got out and stopped to peruse their surroundings. With the toddler on her hip, the woman unlocked the front door. The three entered the house without fanfare and shut the door behind them.

SEVENTH GRADE

Happy chatter filled the halls of Stone Creek Junior High School as three hundred sixth, seventh, and eighth graders flooded into the building. Melody and Kelley stood among their friends, smiling and talking excitedly as they scanned their class assignments and made plans for seating arrangements at lunch. At last the warning bell rang. They had five minutes to get to class, so they slammed their locker doors shut and walked together to their first period—English with Mrs. Cole.

As they entered the room, Melody noticed a new face. There was an empty desk on the second row in front of the new girl, so she plopped her books down and sat, waiting for Kelley to grab the desk to her right. The new girl didn't look up, appearing to be studying her class schedule. She looked tired. Her hair hung in dark waves on both sides of her face, partially obscuring her features but revealing enough to allow Melody to see that she had tan skin and dark eyes framed by thick lashes. Her lips, full and defined by a rim of dark lipliner, were pursed slightly to one side as she seemed to nervously chew the inside of her cheek. Melody ducked down slightly to get into her line of vision and smiled.

"Hi, I'm Melody."

The girl didn't lift her head at first, just raised her eyes to meet Melody's.

"I'm Hannah." Upon seeing Melody's friendly smile, she sat up straight. "I'm new in town."

"Yeah, I figured. Small town, small school. When did you move here?" "Yesterday," said Hannah.

"Really? Where do you live?"

"On Newhope Lane, just about two miles from here."

"Really?" Melody said again—loudly, hopefully. "Me too! I think we live across the street from you! Are you in the house with the pretty gardens out front? The one with the blue trim?"

"Yep, that's the one." Hannah looked down again. "I was hoping for another girl to hang out with."

"Me too! Awesome. We will have to get together really soon." Melody caught Kelley's eye and realized she had temporarily forgotten about her. "Oh! Sorry, this is Kelley. She's my best friend. We've known each other, like, forever."

"Forever," echoed Kelley with a smile. "Hi Hannah."

Hannah looked back and forth between the two girls, obviously relieved to have made new friends so easily. The bell rang and the students quickly took their seats as Mrs. Cole entered the room.

Mrs. Cole was a tall woman, in her fifties, with salt and pepper hair, a bulky frame, and reading glasses dangling from a sparkling chain around her neck. She walked quietly to the front of the room, picked up a piece of chalk, and began to write.

Seventh Grade English Mrs. Cole

"Good morning and welcome to seventh grade English! My name is Carolyn Cole. I hope you are ready to dive in because we are going to have a busy year!"

Lunchtime came quickly. Thank goodness. Melody was starving. She had eaten breakfast, but in her excitement to get to school she had only had a bowl of cereal. It had worn off within an hour, so she was more than ready to sit down to whatever the cafeteria ladies had concocted to mark this first day of the new year.

Pizza. Melody thanked the server behind the glass sneeze guard and stopped at the cashier to pay for her lunch with the money her mother had given her. She found Kelley and sat next to her.

"So far so good, huh?" said Kelley.

"Yeah, except for Math. Mrs. Simpson is all business. I'm afraid I'm going to have a hard time in her class."

"She definitely talks fast," Kelley mumbled as she took a gulp of chocolate milk. "But she seems nice enough."

"I guess," said Melody. She folded her pizza in half and took a big bite. "Mmm, this is good. I was starving. I should've had eggs like my mom suggested this morning."

"You must be hungry if you think this tastes good!" Kelley shook her head and poked at the salad on her plate with a fork.

"Gah, look at this dressing. Watery. Yuck."

Within a few moments Hannah appeared, looking timid.

"Hi again. Um, do you guys mind if I sit with you?"

"Sure!" Both girls spoke at the same time, and Hannah smiled shyly. She slid her lunch tray onto the table and pulled the chair out so she could sit.

"So how is your first day so far?" asked Melody.

"Good. I'm just overwhelmed. I always hate starting a new school," said Hannah.

"Oh, have you moved before?" Melody took another big bite of her pizza.

"Yes, you could say that." Hannah picked up a fork and began to cut her pizza into little squares. "We move almost every other year."

"Really? Is your dad military or something?" asked Kelley.

"No, but his job keeps us moving." Hannah daintily took a bite. She didn't offer more information.

Melody pressed. "What does he do?"

"He works for the government. It's top secret, really. I don't even know the details, but we move a lot."

"Wow . . ." Melody whistled softly. "That's cool. Top secret. Awesome." Kelley nodded, wide-eyed, as her imagination went crazy with images of secret agents and military police casing Hannah's house. Way cool.

"Yeah, so . . . what about you guys?"

Melody giggled. "That's the second time you have said you guys! Where are you from?

"Michigan, why?"

"Because around here we say y'all! Like, 'What about y'all?' We're gonna have to teach you good southern lingo!"

"Oh, okay!" Hannah laughed. "Y'all!"

"Much better," said Melody. "So, my dad is a mechanic. My mom works at a church. She is the secretary."

"What about you?" Hannah asked Kelley. Kelley looked away.

"My mom is looking for a job. Dad left. We don't know where he is." Hannah obviously regretted asking Kelley and looked at her food.

"I'm sorry."

"It's okay. You didn't know." Kelley offered a half-smile and Hannah shrugged.

"Life sucks sometimes. I get that."

Melody was surprised to hear Hannah speak in such an icy tone. So far she had been the epitome of ladylike manners, but Hannah's last statement had an odd edge to it. Melody didn't want to pry, so she moved on to another subject.

"Do you have any brothers or sisters?"

"Yeah, three sisters. I'm the oldest."

"That's great! I can't wait to meet them!"

The three girls continued chatting between bites, keeping the conversation light until the thirty-minute lunch period ended with another ring of the bell. They followed the crowd of kids to the garbage bins that flanked the swinging double doors of the cafeteria, dumping uneaten food into the trash and stacking the trays and silverware on the shelves mounted on the wall above the bins. Melody waved goodbye to Kelley and Hannah and headed downstairs to her next class.

After lunch, Hannah's schedule said she had study hall. She stood outside the cafeteria and looked both ways before walking down the long hall to her left toward the library. As she entered the large room lined with tall shelves filled with hundreds of colorful books, she smiled. The other kids who had the same fourth period assignment were already seated at various long tables, and the librarian busily flipped the pages of a notebook to find her place. Perching on the edge of her desk, she smiled at each seventh grader in turn, waiting for the chatter to settle down. Hannah found an empty chair and sat carefully, trying not to draw attention to herself. The students who shared her table glanced at her curiously before fixing their eyes back on the librarian.

"My name is Miss Keller," she said in a friendly tone, "and you are in the library." A boy across the room snorted. The girl sitting next to him muttered "Duh," and rolled her eyes.

Miss Keller continued. "So this is study hall. Right now you may not realize your need for this hour, but I assure you, as the semester goes on, you will be glad for it. It will free up a lot of time at home if you will take advantage of this time.

I don't mind if you visit with one another, but you must remember a few simple rules: In the library we respect the need for silence for those who do choose to study. That means you have to speak softly at all times. Also, if you have nothing to study—no homework or projects to work on—I will be happy to give you things to do in here. I can always use a little help managing all of this!" She gestured, arms wide, drawing their attention to their surroundings with a flourish of both hands in symmetry.

"There are two computers in the corner that you are welcome to use, as well as three typewriters in the lab through that glass door in the back of the room. The computers do have Oregon Trail loaded, which will be fun for many of you, but do take turns and don't spend all of your time on them. Take advantage of this hour and do your homework!" The girls nearest to Miss Keller giggled. She directed her smile at them. "Any questions?"

The room fell silent and Hannah waited for the signal that they were free to move about the room before getting out of her chair and approaching the shelves marked "Poetry." She tilted her head to the right, perusing book after book, noting unfamiliar titles and quietly mouthing them aloud to herself as she inspected shelf after shelf of plastic-protected volumes.

There. There was a familiar name: Emily Jane Brontë. Hannah gingerly slid the book off the shelf and opened it, letting the pages fall where they may. "Hope" was the title that greeted her eyes, and Hannah began to read:

Hope was but a timid friend;
She sat without the grated den,
Watching how my fate would tend,
Even as selfish-hearted men.
She was cruel in her fear;
Through the bars, one dreary day,
I looked out to see her there,
And she turned her face away!
Like a false guard, false watch keeping,
Still, in strife, she whispered peace;
She would sing while I was weeping;
If I listened, she would cease.
False she was, and unrelenting;
When my last joys strewed the ground,
Even Sorrow saw, repenting,
Those sad relics scattered round;
Hope, whose whisper would have given
Balm to all my frenzied pain,
Stretched her wings, and soared to heaven,
Went, and ne'er returned again!

Hannah shivered. The words hit too close to home. She closed the book quickly and picked up another. Gerard Manley Hopkins. Hmmm, she had never read any of his poetry. Just his name made her smile. She opened to the index and, with her fingertips, traced the titles until she found one that looked promising: "Moonrise." She turned to the correct page and read the words printed there:

Moonless darkness stands between.

Past, the Past, no more be seen!

But the Bethlehem-star may lead me

To the sight of Him Who freed me

From the self that I have been.

Make me pure, Lord: Thou art holy;

Make me meek, Lord: Thou wert lowly;

Now beginning, and alway:

Now begin, on Christmas day.

Hannah pursed her lips, willing her mind to still and her emotions to calm. Freedom was a foreign concept. Her life was anything but free, and she was certain there was not another kid in the school who would understand the reality of her existence —the darkness that enveloped her mind and heart. She was only twelve years old, but she had already died a thousand deaths. She glanced furtively at the others chatting happily around the tables and gathered in a cluster at the computer. Her life depended on the successful performance of a charade of normalcy. Of innocence. No one could know of the demons that haunted her nights and threatened her very soul.

HELLO

Homework was assigned on day one of the new academic year, much to the chagrin of almost every student at Stone Creek Middle School. After the final bell rang, Melody's mother and Jake met her in front of the school, smiling broadly.

"How was your first day of seventh grade?" she asked as they crossed the busy parking lot.

"It was really good. I met a new girl! Her family is the one that moved in across the street!"

"That's wonderful! What is her name?"

"Hannah," said Melody. "And she has sisters! It will be fun having a girl so close to home to hang out with."

Melody tossed her backpack onto the floor before climbing into the front passenger seat. Jake was settled in his normal spot behind her, fishing around in his backpack for a Jolly Rancher, which he unwrapped and tossed into his mouth. Allie started the engine, backing out as the kids chattered about their day. She asked more about Hannah and her family and determined to reach out to them as soon as she could whip up a batch of cookies. After they pulled into the driveway, Melody and Jake raced inside to grab a snack. Allie opened the refrigerator and popped the tops on two cans of Coke, handing one to each of the kids. After they finished their snacks, Melody sat down at the kitchen table to do her homework, and Jake disappeared into his bedroom.

"Mom, after I finish this can I go across the street to Hannah's?"

"Why don't you give me about thirty minutes to bake some cookies to take with us? I think that would be a nice way to introduce ourselves to them," said Allie.

"Okay. I'll work while you cook. And then I'll sample one just to be sure they're not poisonous," Melody said with a wink at her mom. "Wouldn't want to kill the neighbors, right?"

"Right," said Allie with a grin and an exaggerated wink back at her daughter.

Half an hour later, Allie arranged two dozen chocolate chip cookies on a disposable foil pie plate and covered them with plastic wrap. Melody knocked on Jake's door, telling him they were going across the street. After sampling two cookies and deeming them to be neighbor- worthy, Melody and her mother walked the short distance to the new neighbors' house and rang the doorbell.

Heavy footsteps neared and then the sound of a chain lock sliding just preceded the opening of the wooden door. A well-dressed man with olive skin and dark, straight hair slicked back off his brow emerged. He was not a tall man, just a little taller than Allie, who was five foot seven.

"Hello," he said in a deep, raspy baritone voice. His eyes held no expression.

"Hello! We are the Greens. We live just across the street," said Allie cheerfully. "My daughter met your daughter today at school, I believe. We wanted to welcome you to the neighborhood."

She trailed off, looking down at the platter in her hand. The man didn't respond.

"Um, these are for you. I hope you like chocolate chips!" Allie held the platter out to him.

"Thank you. They look delicious." The man smiled slightly, which made him seem a little more relaxed. A little girl, about two years old, suddenly appeared behind him. She did not smile but stared at them as she held onto his left leg.

"Oh! What a cutie!" Melody exclaimed. "What's your name?"

The man looked down at the girl and she looked at him, wide-eyed. She continued to hold his leg and he bent down to pry her loose, shooing her back as he stepped outside and closed the door behind him.

"She is supposed to be napping," he said. He looked at Melody. "Hannah told me about you. She was happy to have a friend. She is busy right now but I will let her know you stopped by." His ebony eyes shifted their focus back to Allie. "Thank you for the cookies," he said as Allie placed the plate in his hands. The corners of his mouth turned up very slightly. Allie took that for another smile.

"You are very welcome!" Allie said. "I'm sure things are crazy right now with unpacking and all, but please let us know if you need anything. And when you get settled in we'd love to meet the rest of your family."

"Thank you," he said. "I will keep that in mind."

Allie nodded and put her hand on Melody's arm as they turned around to walk back to their house. The man went back inside and closed the door behind him.

"Well, that was weird," said Melody after they went inside.

"What do you mean?" asked her mother.

"He didn't even tell us his name!"

"You know, you are right! Goodness, how did we manage to forget to ask his name?"

Allie shook her head, frustrated with herself.

"Probably because of the little girl. Is she cute or what? Those curls—she looks like a blonde Little Orphan Annie!"

"Yes, she does. She is beautiful. And so shy! Maybe she knew she was in trouble for getting up from her nap." Allie smiled, remembering when her children were nap-fighting toddlers. "We will give them a few days to get things in order, then invite them over."

From behind the heavy living room curtain—that were to always be closed—the man watched Melody and her mother go into their house before walking down the dark hall to find Hannah. She was in the room she shared with Rosie, Jessie, and Leslie. Jessie was sitting next to Leslie on the floor in front of their dollhouse. Sprawled across her bed with a book open before her, Hannah looked up as he entered without knocking, still holding Rosie's hand. When he released the toddler she ran across the room to join the girls in front of the dollhouse, climbing onto Leslie's lap and sticking her thumb in her mouth.

"You made a friend today. That's good. If things go well this week maybe you can earn time to spend with her." He looked at Jessie. "You should be asleep, Jessie."

"I can't sleep, Papa. I'm not tired."

"Well, you will be, so you need to lie down. I'll give you something to help. I can't have you showing up to school with circles under your eyes this soon." Jessie looked down at the Ken doll in her hand. She took a deep breath, which Hannah noticed.

"Hey, Jess, you want me to lay next to you?" Jessie nodded,

still looking at her doll. "Okay, come on."

Hannah motioned for Jessie to join her on the twin bed. The springs creaked as the girls settled into the soft mattress, Hannah holding her sister from behind and humming softly as the man went to the bathroom to get a medicine bottle. He poured some into a small dosing cup and gave it to Jessie, who drank it quickly. He left without a word, closing the door behind him as Hannah continued to hum until she felt Jessie relax in her arms and fall asleep.

Her mind drifted back to the school day, to Melody and Kelley. Oh, how she hoped she could make this work. She wanted real friends her age so badly. Her family's last assignment had been so lonely, living out in the country and no neighbors anywhere nearby. Papa's job suddenly uprooted them, as usual, and the girls were excited when they found out they were moving into a neighborhood in town.

Hannah looked at the clock on the wall. She carefully got up and went to the bathroom, getting the medicine Papa had given Jessie and measuring out a dose for herself. It was always better this way. She crawled under her pink and white comforter, the lace edging tickling her chin as she burrowed down, and waited for sleep to come.

ADJUSTING

It was the first weekend of the school year. Throughout the week Melody, Kelley, and Hannah had spent every lunch period together. Melody and Kelley were drawn to Hannah's laid-back manner and quick wit right away. She was an interesting person with a lot of stories to tell from the many places she had lived. Melody and Kelley loved to listen to her and found themselves laughing easily as she recounted tales of travel, crazy neighbors, and rural life. She seemed to have lived a thousand years to their twelve, and they quickly felt quite honored to be her friends as word spread throughout the seventh grade of the cool new student.

Maybe popularity was within reach for these girls who had, so far, lived such ordinary lives. Being associated with someone who had lived real adventures seemed to be raising them a notch or two on the social ladder already.

Saturday found the three of them sitting in the shade of the mimosa tree by the road in Melody's front yard. The tree's broad canopy brought relief from the hot September sun. A battery-operated radio was nestled in the patchy grass and they talked about the week's events as music played in the background.

"So what do you think of Mrs. Cole?" asked Melody.

"I like her. Caleb had her when he was in seventh grade, and she was nice," said Kelley. "Me, too," said Melody. "What about you, Hannah? Do you like her?"

"Yeah, I think so. I am just not a big fan of writing. Essays, book reports . . . yuck. I'm no good at that stuff."

"You just don't like it, or is it hard for you?" Melody hoped the question didn't offend Hannah.

"I just don't like it. Those creative writing assignments . . . ugh. Not my thing."

Kelley spoke: "But you are so good at telling stories! I would think you would love writing! Shoot, I haven't heard so many different stories from anyone in my whole life! Except for maybe my Granny V . . ."

"Well, it's one thing to tell stories about other people. Even reading is great to me—an escape from real life. But it's a whole other thing to have to talk about your own stuff," said Hannah. "Anyway, no biggie. I'll get through it. I always do."

"I can't imagine you having a lot of stuff to tell about yourself. You seem . . . normal," said Melody with a mischievous grin.

"Yeah, normal! I'll let you think that!" Hannah laughed. "Who decides what is normal, anyway?"

"No joke," said Kelley. "I have no idea what normal is anymore."

"What's wrong, Kel?" Melody looked at her friend with concern.

"Nothing. Nothing new, anyway. Mama was just on a tear last night. The older boys got caught trespassing on Mr. Barrett's land and he ran them off. I guess he called her and threatened to call the police next time. She just lost it completely, crying about what would happen if they ended up in jail. They yelled at her and acted like she was crazy and she ended up shutting herself in her room. She wouldn't let any of us in." Kelley shrugged then sighed hard. "Sorry, I didn't intend to bring us all down."

Hannah took a deep breath and smiled sympathetically. "We all have our downers, right? I'm sorry. I guess I kind of started the downward turn. Let's change the subject. What are you guys doing tomorrow?"

"You guys?" Melody playfully turned, putting her hands on Hannah's shoulders and shaking her gently. "It's y'all around here, honey! You've gotta remember that or you'll get laughed out of town!"

"Okay, y'all!" Hannah exaggerated the Texas drawl of her friends. "So what are y'all doing tomorrow?"

"I plan on hanging out at my Grandparents'. That's my usual Sunday routine," said Kelley.

"I have to go to church in the morning. After that I don't have plans," said Mel.

"Church? Ooh, painful. I went to church once. They tried to drown me. Never went back," said Hannah with a grin.

"Ha ha, very funny." Melody squinted playfully at Hannah. "I actually like it. We've always gone, and I have a lot of friends there. Maybe you should come sometime. I promise they won't throw you in the baptistry!"

"No thanks," said Hannah. "I need my beauty sleep."

"You could come hang out with me at Granny V's if you want," offered Kelley. Melody's eyes darted involuntarily to her friend, a twinge of jealousy cutting at her heart.

Granny V's? Without her? Suddenly she felt like a third wheel. She fought the ugly emotion that threatened her, and swallowed hard.

"I'll think about it," said Hannah. "Want me to call you when I wake up? If you're still home then I can meet up with you."

"Okay, cool!" Kelley looked at Melody then, sensitive to her best friend's feelings and not wanting her to think she was being left out. "You could come after church if you want."

"I might," said Melody coolly. She mentally kicked herself for being petty then intentionally softened her tone. "I mean, I'll call when I get home . . . after lunch, okay?"

Kelley smiled at Melody and looked back at Hannah. "You will love my grandmother. She is awesome. Totally fun."

"Yeah, I'm sure. I haven't ever been around grandmas, so I guess this will be a first, huh?"

"You don't have grandparents?" asked Kelley.

"Nope. They died before I was born. No grandparents, no aunts and uncles. Just whoever we happen to get to know whenever we move."

"That sounds . . . lonely." Kelley couldn't imagine life with no extended family, especially her grandparents.

"I've never known any different. But I have my sisters."

"And your parents," said Melody.

"Yeah, them too."

Sunday morning began with a bang. A loud peal of thunder awakened Melody an hour before she would have needed to get up for church. She lay in bed for a few minutes, willing her pounding heart to slow down, and hoping to go back to sleep. A flash lit up her room, followed three seconds later by another deafening crack of thunder that seemed to shake the house. Within minutes, rain arrived. The sky opened up and it poured down heavily upon the little town.

Melody pulled her blue floral bedspread over her head and willed her ears to stop working, but another boom made her jump, and she finally gave up and pulled herself into a sitting position, her long legs dangling off the side of her bed. She looked at the clock and stood, reaching for her robe, which was draped over the back of her desk chair. She put it on, pulling her long hair out from beneath the collar, and stumbled out of the room.

"Mom?"

"I'm in here, honey." Her mother sat alone in the living room with the television on. "I'm watching the weather report. There is nothing to worry about. Just a storm."

"Okay, good." Melody sat on the sofa next to her mom, leaning against her and breathing in the scent of her mom's freshly shampooed hair. "That thunder was loud. I nearly had a heart attack."

"I figured it would wake you. Thank goodness we are not in tornado season, right?"

"For real." Melody yawned and sank a little deeper into the soft sofa. "I could have used that extra hour of sleep."

"I know. But I guess we will just have plenty of time to get ready. Hungry?" "I guess."

"Want some pancakes?"

"Sure. Want me to wake Jacob?"

"You can wait a little while. He won't take long to get ready."

"Okay." Melody shook her head. It never ceased to amaze her how Jake could sleep through anything. "Where's Dad?"

"He was sitting on the bed with the newspaper a few minutes ago. I figure he is about to get in the shower."

"Well, I'll go get dressed . . . unless you want me to help you."

"No, I've got it under control, sweetie. Thanks. You get dressed and I'll have breakfast ready in a jiffy!" Allie stood and bent down to kiss the top of her daughter's head. "Love you."

"Love you, too."

After pancakes and bacon, the Greens piled into the minivan to drive to church. Thankfully, the storm had passed quickly and the clouds were moving on. As they pulled into the parking lot, Melody spotted Sarah Miller. She waved and hurriedly jumped out of the van as soon as it came to a complete stop, running over to walk up the white stone steps with her.

"Hi! How was your first week of classes?" asked Melody.

"Great!" Sarah smiled broadly and gave Melody a quick side hug. "You like seventh grade?"

"Yeah, it's good so far." She watched Sarah shake hands with Pastor Roger and hug his wife, Mrs. Dixon. Sarah was a few years older than Melody but they had grown up going to church together. Sarah always took time to talk to Melody, which made Melody feel very special. She loved being around Sarah, who was not only beautiful, with her long blonde hair and blue eyes, but was also extremely kind.

"Great! Who did you get for English?"

"Mrs. Cole."

"Oh, you will love her. She was my favorite teacher. I never knew diagramming could be so much fun until I had her!"

"Diagramming? Fun?" Melody laughed. "You're kidding!"

"Nope. She turned it into a game. Kind of like uncovering clues. You'll see." Sarah smiled. "She is awesome."

The girls walked through the foyer toward the wing of the church where the youth group met each week. Sarah gave Melody another quick side hug and told her she'd see her after Sunday school, then darted into the high school classroom. Melody walked to the next room down the hall where the middle school class met and found a seat next to Corey Michaelson, who was also in her English class at school. She smiled at Corey, who nodded back with a shy smile and pushed her glasses back into place, as the youth leader, Barry Gales, took his position on a stool behind the music-stand-turned-podium in the front of the room.

"Hey guys! Welcome! Grab a seat and we'll get started!" The noise died down immediately and Barry sat on the stool behind the music stand. "I hope you all had a good first week of school. I'm glad you made it here today because we have some great stuff to talk about. A new school year means a new study, and we are going to dive deep into this one. You'll love it."

Barry reached behind him and picked up a stack of thin books. He stood and began to walk from one person to another, giving each a book.

"Anyone ever read the book of Romans?" Corey Michaelson and a boy in the back of the room raised their hands. "Good! Okay, well, by the time we finish this study—if you do your homework—you will all have read the book. This book, guys, is awesome. It is life-changing if you will let it be. I can't wait to get started." Barry gave out the last book and walked back to the front of the room, perching on the edge of the stool.

"All right, here we go. Let me start by reading the first few verses: 'Paul, a servant of Christ Jesus, called to be an apostle and set apart for the gospel of God. . . .'"

Melody listened and took an occasional note as Barry spoke. He was so engaging and he made understanding the Bible seem so easy. Time passed quickly and soon Melody was sitting beside her mother, father, and Jake in the sanctuary with hymnals open while Mrs. Miller, Sarah's mother, played the piano. The words were familiar, having been sung regularly in this church her entire life. She sang along, her mother's beautiful alto voice harmonizing with hers:

A pilgrim was I, and a wand'ring,
In the cold night of sin I did roam

When Jesus the kind Shepherd found me,

And now I am on my way home.

After the closing song and final prayer was offered, the congregants poured out of the church into the bright September sun. Melody and her family went home to a kitchen filled with the smell of pot roast, carrots, and potatoes, along with homemade yeast rolls.

"Mm-mm! Now that smells good!" Melody's father slapped his belly in anticipation as Allie opened up the cabinet to take out plates and glasses.

"Here, Mel. Set the table for me, please." Melody obliged and placed the items carefully on their small dining table while Jake obeyed his mother's command to wash his hands. Soon they were all seated, grace was said, and the room fell quiet as mouths were busy chewing.

"Honey, you've done it again. Delicious!" Pete took another bite of pot roast and closed his eyes in mock ecstasy.

"Thank you," Allie smiled at her husband. "I'm glad you all like it."

Melody spoke up: "I'm supposed to go over to Granny V's with Kelley and Hannah."

"Oh! Well, that sounds like fun. But I'd rather you not rush through lunch."

"I'm not. I just told them I'd come after lunch." Melody took another bite. "This will be the first time Hannah has met her."

"Well, I have no doubt she will love Violet."

"Yeah, no doubt. Everyone does." Melody looked away, focusing for a second on the trees swaying outside in the wind. "Is it supposed to rain again?"

"You know, I think it is. Why don't I drive you over there, honey? I don't want you to get caught in a storm. I can just plan on picking you up later. And if Hannah needs a ride home I can get her as well."

"Okay." Melody put her fork down. "I'd like that. You know how much I hate storms."

SOMETHING

Violet sat on her sofa, a lit cigarette perched on the brown glass ashtray balanced on the upholstered arm. The TV flickered across the small room, but Violet wasn't paying attention to what was on the screen.

Something wasn't right.

She couldn't put her finger on it, but the feeling was there. Gnawing. Troubling. Kelley had brought over a new friend—Hannah. The girl seemed nice enough, but there was something about her. Something in her countenance. Hannah was full of stories and laughter, but the laughter did not reach her eyes. She was polite and well-mannered, and Violet could tell that Kelley really enjoyed being with her, but Violet could not help but feel there was more to Hannah than met the eye.

Melody had come over after lunch and Violet intentionally stepped back and left the three girls to have their fun while she watched from a distance. Kelley and Melody had their typical mannerisms, the throwing-their-head-back laughter and easy hugs. Hannah, though very talkative, seemed to hold back. She didn't let loose like the two old friends did. She kept her distance physically.

Maybe it was because she was new. Violet shook her head, willing the feeling to go away. This was silly. Of course Hannah was reserved. She had just moved to Parkland and had just met these girls a little over a week ago. It would take time for her to loosen up and relax. But still, there was something that felt out of place. It lurked behind Hannah's eyes. She reminded Violet of what some referred to as an old soul, wise to the world in a way not typical of most twelve-year-olds. Hannah was careful. Too careful.

Violet looked out the window at the gathering storm clouds. She was glad Melody's mother had picked her and Hannah up before the storm hit. After the friends had gone home, Kelley had come back over to Violet's trailer to join her grandparents for dinner. She had left about an hour ago, going back home to do homework and prepare for school the next day.

Violet got up, walked across the room, and turned up the volume on the television as the meteorologist gave the nine o'clock weather report. It looked like the storm would be here for a couple of hours. She glanced out her kitchen window and could see Kelley sitting at her kitchen table with her mother. Nora was sewing a button onto a shirt while Kelley talked. Good. She was glad to see those girls looking relaxed for once.

Oh, how she wished their lives were easier. How she wished she could take away the pain that always hovered just under the surface in Nora's heart, bleeding out onto her children.

The rain started to fall. It sprinkled the ground softly at first, then gathered strength as lightning lit up the evening sky and thunder shook the little trailer house. Violet looked up at the ceiling and whispered a prayer. She prayed for her daughter and granddaughter.

And she prayed for Hannah.

IN DISGUISE

The semester wore on and the students of Stone Creek Junior High settled into their routines. Homework, band practice, academic clubs, and sports all consumed the afternoons of the kids and helped to keep them out of trouble.

Most of the time.

As the end of October neared, thoughts turned toward Halloween. Many conversations hovered around what each student wanted to wear for the big night. Local churches offered alternatives for those who would rather not walk the neighborhood streets, and costume stores popped up in otherwise empty buildings with an odd assortment of masks and often-gory costumes in their windows.

Melody, Kelley, and Hannah decided it would be fun to spend Halloween together. They had spent many an afternoon the past two months under the big mimosa in Melody's yard, and their friendship had grown closer.

Today was one week before Halloween and the girls were sitting together, as usual, in the school cafeteria during lunch.

"What are you going to wear?" asked Kelley through a

mouthful of bologna and mayo on white bread.

"I've had a hard time deciding this year," said Melody. "We are getting too old to trick or treat, I guess. I wasn't even sure if I should dress up, but I suppose I could help my mom hand out candy."

"You don't have a costume?" Kelley was surprised. Of course, she didn't either. There was no way her mom could afford to buy a costume.

"Well, I have some stuff I could put together—you know, like, maybe dress like Michael Jackson."

Kelley laughed out loud. "Oh my gosh, Mel! Are you serious? You totally should do that. Get a curly wig and you could moonwalk to the front door to give out candy!"

Melody grinned. Her mother often said she never ceased to be amazed at her daughter's love for pop music. Photos cut from magazines lined the inside of her locker, and her favorite album, like millions of other fans, was Thriller.

"I have a white glove, black shoes, and white socks. My mom said she could spray glitter on them. And my brother has a red jacket I can wear, with zippers, like in the 'Beat It' video."

"Awesome!" Kelley's eyes sparkled.

"What about you, Kel?"

The sparkle faded. "What do you think?" she asked, begrudgingly.

"Well, if I'm Michael Jackson, shouldn't you be Madonna? My mom has junk jewelry and I'm sure your mom has old lace in her sewing box, right? We could throw that look together in no time!"

Kelley's eyes brightened again, inspired by Melody's idea.

"Will you help me? You are so much better at stuff like this than I am." "Of course! It will be fun!"

Both girls suddenly realized Hannah had not joined the conversation. After a half-second pause, Melody asked Hannah what she planned to wear.

"It's a secret." Hannah face was expressionless. "I wouldn't want anyone to steal my idea."

"Oh, come on!" both girls said in unison.

"Nope, I'm not telling." She raised one eyebrow and smiled a seductive smile before she winked. "You'll see soon enough. It will be memorable. My costumes always are."

HALLOWEEN

In the fading light of dusk, children happily chattered as they walked door to door. Barbies, super heroes, angels, firefighters, and princesses peered through oddly-placed eye holes in their plastic masks, and a muffled "Trick or treat!" greeted the open doors of friendly neighbors. Melody, Kelley, and Hannah had planned to meet by the mimosa tree. They were really too old to go trick or treating, but having a night to wander the neighborhood freely was fun. Besides, they could rob their younger siblings' candy stashes later.

Kelley arrived at the tree just a few minutes after Melody. They both burst into giggles when they laid eyes on each other. Melody was a girlish Michael Jackson—red jacket, white glove and all. She struck a pose and Kelley burst out laughing. Kelley was a cute Madonna. Hair teased, lace around her wrists, short skirt, and long strands of plastic beads layered around her neck.

"You look awesome!" Melody said with a big smile. "What did your mom think?"

"She hasn't seen it. She was asleep when I left. But Granny V thought it was great, except she said she wished my skirt was a little longer." Kelley raised her eyebrows. "I guess I can't be surprised at that, huh?"

"Aw, it's not bad. You are a great Madonna!"

"So, where is Hannah?" asked Kelley.

"She should be here any minute. Wait, I think she is coming out now."

Both girls eyes widened as Hannah stepped out of her house. She was dressed like . . . What was she, anyway? Melody's mind scrambled. Hannah was in a floor-length gown made of white fabric with tiny green flowers printed all over. The ruffled top was off the shoulder, trimmed in lace. The bodice was scooped, very low-cut and tight, revealing her maturing body in a very adult manner, and the full skirt, held aloft by a huge petticoat, ended in a ruffled edge with green ribbon accenting the ruffle. She wore a large straw hat, held securely by a wide green ribbon tied under her chin in a perfect bow. Her long brown hair was up in pin curls, peeking out from under the hat, with a few curls escaping at the nape of her neck. She looked much, much older.

"What the heck?" Kelley spoke almost involuntarily. "Where did you get that?"

Hannah spun around, letting her skirt twirl. "My mother ordered it. What do you think?" Melody struggled to find words. "It's, um. Well, it looks like, uh . . ."

"You look like a grown woman." Kelley's words filled in Melody's gaps. "I mean, good grief, Hannah! Who knew you had boobs?"

Hannah laughed. "It's the corset. It pushes everything up. It enhances, you know?"

Hannah raised her eyebrows suggestively as she ran her palms down her side, accenting her curves and looking around to see if anyone on the street had noticed her.

Melody shook her head in disbelief, blinking. "Nope, I don't say I do." She glanced down at her flat chest hidden under the red-zippered jacket. "I look like a dork next to you."

"No you don't—you look like Michael!" Hannah smiled re-assuringly. "I think you look cool! And, Kelley, the Madonna outfit is awesome."

Kelley shifted, trying to find the confidence within her that she saw in Hannah. "Yeah. Thanks."

"So, where do we start?" Hannah could see the hesitation in her friends' eyes, and she didn't want them to bail on her. She knew her costume was different. She knew they had no idea why she would wear something so obviously sexy. She had better be careful so as not to arouse their curiosity any more than she already had. She didn't want to lose this chance at finally having friends her age.

Yeah, she'd better play her cards right.

"Let's go down to the street and see who's out. Mom is with Jake, so we can catch up with them and maybe score some candy."

The girls began to walk. Hannah was fully aware of the stares from families on the street. Little girls thought she was a princess, pointing and smiling. Mothers smiled nervously while fathers fought to keep their eyes on their kids. Well, most of them did. A few openly gawked. Hannah kept her eyes straight ahead, pretending not to notice, though she was fully aware that the hourglass shape created by the tight corset underneath her dress was an attention-getter. Deep inside, she hated it, but had no choice but to push down the lump that threatened to form in her throat.

She had a job to do. Father said she was special. Important. That not just anyone could do what she does. He said she was one of the best in this business. Gifted, even. Her sisters were looking to her for how to live this lifestyle well, and if she failed it could ruin any chance she had at normal friendships and possibly cause them to have to move again.

Hannah was tired of moving.

She lifted her skirt to avoid getting it dirty and tried to engage in normal conversation. The three girls wandered the streets of the neighborhood and stopped occasionally to talk to friends from school or church. After about an hour Melody spotted Sarah Miller and waved. Sarah smiled and crossed the street to talk to Melody.

"Hi! How's it going, Melody?"

"Good, thanks." Melody looked down at Sarah's little sister, Samantha. "Hey Sammie! Are you having fun?"

Five-year-old Samantha smiled shyly. She was dressed in white with a silver halo made of metallic pipe cleaners atop her black, tightly curled hair, which was pulled up into two identical pom-poms. White feathered wings attached by loops around her shoulders bounced behind her as she walked. They contrasted beautifully with Sammie's ebony skin—the legacy of her birthmother who had entrusted her to the Millers just after Sammie was born. Her story was one that moved the hearts of everyone who knew and loved her.

"You look adorable. Cutest angel ever!" Melody reached out and brushed her hand across the top of Samantha's hair. "I bet you are getting more candy than anyone!"

"Actually, I was just taking her over to the church," Sarah said. "They are having a fall festival and we are going to play games and get candy there. Right?" Sarah smiled down at her sister.

"Yeah, and I'm gonna bob for apples!" Sammy clapped her hands together with excitement. "You wanna come too?"

Melody looked at Kelley and Hannah. Kelley shrugged. A look of panic crossed Hannah's face.

"To the church?" Her eyes darted back and forth, looking quickly at the shadows growing as the sun set. "Well, I can't. Sorry. I have to be home by nine. My parents are throwing a party and I have to be there. You two can go if you want." Hannah gave a small smile and turned to walk home before her friends could ask any more questions.

Darkness enveloped the little house as Hannah opened the front door and stepped inside. She crept down the hall to her bedroom, hearing the voices of Carl and Miranda coming from theirs. Their tones were hushed, hurried. The rustling of clothing as Mama changed into her finest dress accompanied the sound of music playing softly in the living room. Hannah sat on the edge of her bed and tried to shake off the feeling of impending doom that always threatened her before these events.

Papa said these parties were a crucial part of their business. They only held them a couple of times each year, and he said they were what kept their business alive and healthy and ensured the family could all stay together. He said what their family did for a living was incredibly unique, so much so that it must never be shared with anyone outside of their household. Hannah, at twelve, was beginning to struggle with the logic of this, though. Why would something so important need to be secret?

Rosie came toddling in, smiling. She had on a frilly white dress with layers of tulle and lace bouncing around her chubby legs. Her blonde hair hung in ringlets past her shoulders, held back with a bright red bow. Hannah scooped her up onto her lap and nuzzled her hair. She was so cute, so innocent.

So unaware.

"Hannah! I wanna eat!" Rosie could obviously smell the appetizers being prepared in the kitchen.

"We can't, Rosie. Remember we have to wait until the guests leave. I can get you a little snack, though, as long as you don't get it on your dress. How about an apple?"

"Okay." Rosie took Hannah by the hand and giggled as she practically dragged her down the hall toward the kitchen.

"Hi Lucya," said Hannah to the old Russian woman at the counter who was arranging bite-sized goodies on a platter.

"Hello little ones!" Lucya smiled broadly, her weathered face brightening as she addressed the girls in her thick accent. She continued her task, hurriedly completing the arrangement and moving to the next empty platter. "I see you are all dressed up! It is going to be a good night, no? Yes, I think it will be."

"Mmm," mumbled Hannah as she reached around Lucya to take an apple out of a large bowl of fruit. "Here, Rose. Want me to cut it up for you?" Rosie nodded and Hannah opened the knife drawer to pull out a small paring knife. She peeled the apple and cored it before cutting it into wedges and handing them one by one to Rosie, who devoured them.

As Rosie swallowed her last bite, their five-year-old sister, Leslie, walked into the kitchen. She was dolled up in a fluffy, pageant-style dress made of pink taffeta. She scratched uncomfortably at her side. "I hate this dress. It is itchy." She scowled at Hannah, apparently hoping she would tell her to go change. But Hannah knew the drill.

"It's just for a couple of hours. You'll be okay. You know you have to wear what they tell you to things like this."

Leslie scowled more deeply. "But I hate it. It's ugly and stupid-looking and it feels awful."

"I'm sorry." Hannah understood Leslie's frustrations. She had been in the same type of outfit many times herself as a little girl, but she learned that if she cooperated she would always be rewarded with treats and playtime. If she didn't, well . . .

Hannah shook her head to clear the unwanted thoughts and smiled at the five-year-old. "Remember, tomorrow you will get to play outside for a little while. Just think about how good the sunshine will feel! It will be fun." Yes, Hannah had become very good at diversions.

"Girls! Do you realize the time?" Mama entered the room in a swoosh of fuchsia. Her low-cut dress showed off her well-proportioned body, and the slit up the left side revealed a muscular, tan thigh. "The guests are making their way over now! Be ready!"

On cue, Lucya turned and handed a tray of appetizers to Hannah and Jessie who had just followed Mama into the kitchen. The two older girls walked into the living room, putting on their game faces. Serious, interested, curious, giving. Yes—all of these qualities must be shown to the guests. The guests must be made to feel sought after, important, worthy. After all, through the magic of the newly-available internet and the anonymity it afforded, some of the top officials in local government had access to invitations to these private events. Mayors, the chief of police, state representatives and senators: these were important, powerful people. It was an honor to be asked to entertain them.

At least, that is what the girls were taught.

Carl suddenly filled the doorway with his dark presence and looked at the girls. His smile was cold, not reaching his eyes.

"It's time. Take your places. Smile."

The girls nodded, including Mama. A quiet knock was heard and Papa opened the back door.

"Welcome."

No one in the neighborhood noticed the patrons trickling in and out of the house, alternating, every thirty minutes. The alley was dark and no cars were parked directly in front of the house. The busy streets on this Halloween night were the perfect disguise for the evil taking place on New Hope Lane. Trick or treaters' knocks and doorbell rings were ignored. All lights on the front of the house were turned off and the windows blacked to prevent the presence of the people inside from being made obvious from the street. Darkness enveloped this house more completely than anyone around them could ever fathom —darkness that threatened souls, scarred hearts, and injured young bodies. Darkness that seemed impenetrable.

Hours later, only the sound of soft weeping could be heard from the girls' rooms as the final patron joined the last of the trick or treaters and walked, unnoticed, to a car parked at the end of the alley. He drove for over an hour, home to his wife, and slipped into bed next to her, turning his back to her silent form as he fell into a fitful and tormented sleep.

A NEW DAY

Hannah awakened late the next morning. She stood on her bed carefully to keep from waking Jessie, who had sought comfort next to Hannah after the party, leaving Leslie alone in the twin bed they usually shared. Hannah pushed the heavy curtains to one side and sunlight streamed through, causing her to squint. She turned and looked at Rose curled up in her crib. She was just beginning to stir. Tear streaks were dried onto Jessie's cheeks. Rosie was sucking her thumb. Hannah's stomach turned at the sight of blood on Rosie's sheet. She ran to the bathroom and vomited.

Oh, God, how she had hoped Rose would be allowed to wait a little longer. She was only two. She grasped the side of the toilet and fought back sobs. Why was this suddenly so hard? This is how her family had always made their living. Why was it bothering her so much now? It was seeing sweet, innocent Rose lying there in the aftermath of what had been forced upon her that was stirring something in her gut that she was having a very difficult time pushing back down. When Jessie first began working, Hannah was only nine and had a separate bedroom. They lived in Idaho that year—in the sticks. No neighbors, certainly no friends to compare lives with. Their world was very small; they only socialized within their household between events and never interacted socially with their classmates at school for fear of being asked questions they could not answer. Carl had trained them thoroughly to avoid friendships.

Now, life was different. After another isolated stint in Michigan, an hour and a half from the nearest town, they were in a neighborhood for the very first time in their lives. They were allowed to go to a school with lots of kids and actually have friends that they could visit outside of their classrooms. Living in the middle of nowhere had finally panned itself out, and patrons had stopped making the drive. They needed to be in society and they needed to be accessible, especially to those who made last-minute arrangements and did not desire to drive long distances on dark country roads late at night.

For the first time Hannah had actual friends. She was seeing a difference in the way Melody and Kelley lived—a carefree air that she had never experienced before. An innocence that she had never known. Even Kelley's difficult family situation didn't completely dampen her fun-loving spirit. It appealed to Hannah so deeply that she could not shake it. It created a longing within her that she was having a very difficult time ignoring.

She cleaned up the toilet and changed out of her pajamas into a pair of jeans and a light green sweater. Walking into the kitchen, she saw Carl. He looked up from his coffee and smiled, a straight, thin stretching of his weathered lips as he lifted a cigarette and sucked on it while winking coldly.

"Good work last night. You made a lot of people very happy."

Hannah nodded and went to the refrigerator. She took out the jug of milk and got a glass out of the upper cabinet. Papa watched her closely. She could feel his eyes on her back. She allowed herself to admit she hated him.

"After I eat can I go to Melody's?"

He set his cup down and rustled the newspaper spread across the table, turning the page. "Yes. You earned it."

"Thanks." Hannah tore a banana from the rest of the bunch and peeled it, taking a bite and walking out the front door. She breathed deeply, relishing the fresh air, and went across the street to the Greens' house.

Melody and Hannah sat under the Mimosa tree, eating home-baked cinnamon rolls made by Melody's mom. Hannah was growing more and more comfortable with Allie, loving her gentle demeanor and welcoming manner. She made Hannah feel . . . valued. Melody was filling Hannah in on the fall festival at her church. She and Kelley had joined Sarah Miller for the rest of the evening and it had apparently been a blast.

Good, clean fun.

"So, how was your party?" asked Melody.

"My party? Oh, it was fine. It was just a thing for clients of my father. I guess you would call it a meet and greet." Hannah shrugged, hoping Melody would change the subject.

"What did you have to do? It stinks that you couldn't go with us and had to hang out with a bunch of adults."

So much for changing the subject.

"Well, my father wanted his clients to meet the whole family. My sister and I helped serve food. We are used to it. He has these things periodically. But today I'm free as a bird." Hannah grinned halfheartedly. "So!" She jumped up, determined to change the subject this time. "What is Kelley up to?"

"I haven't talked to her yet today. Wanna call her?"

"Yeah, let's."

The girls stood up and stretched, wiping grass off their bottoms and picking up the empty plates to take inside. They entered the front door and Melody walked around the Formica island jutting out from the kitchen wall and picked up the phone, stepping slowly across the kitchen after she dialed Kelley's phone number, the coils of the long cord stretching and sagging across the room. She came to a stop in front of the sink, leaning back against the counter and crossing her ankles.

The phone on the other end rang three times, then Kelley answered.

"Hey Kel! It's Melody. Got any plans today?"

"I do now! Give me twenty minutes and I'll be there, okay?"

"Sounds good." Melody smiled at Hannah. "Want us to meet you halfway?"

"Sure! See you in a few minutes." Kelley hung up the phone and yelled for her Mom.

Nora emerged from her bedroom, an unlit cigarette in her hand. "I'm going to Melody's."

"Okay," said Nora. "Just be sure you are home by dinner. I'm cooking for once!" Kelley smiled, glad to see her mother in a more upbeat mood.

"Got it." Kelley grabbed her shoes that were strewn on the floor in front of the sofa and darted out the screen door, letting it slam with a bang behind her. Across the lawn, Granny V sat on the bottom step of her front porch.

"Hi baby girl! Where are you goin'?" Her raspy voice made Kelley smile.

"To Melody's. I'll be back by dinner. Mama's cooking!"

Violet raised her eyebrows in sincere surprise, then waved Kelley on with a wrinkled hand. "Have fun!"

The three girls met halfway, exchanged hugs, and walked together back to Melody's house. They talked and laughed and shared stories about friends and school and siblings. At least, two of them did. Hannah, though, forced herself to hold back. She knew not to tell too much, not to encourage any curiosity about her family. Hannah's goal today was to preserve these friendships that had suddenly become very important to her.

She kept the focus on her friends, enjoying their lighthearted banter and imagining that her life was just as normal as theirs. Something deep inside told her that these girls walking beside her were necessary to her emotional well-being.

Maybe even to her survival.

Hannah tried not to think about Rosie, Leslie, or Jessie. Not right now. Just pretend for a while.

She looked at Melody and Kelley through fresh eyes today. If you asked her, she could not have put into words why. The girls were completely unaware of the awakening that had begun inside their newest friend. They had no way of knowing how abnormal their normalcy was in her life, how a spark had been lit inside Hannah's soul that would refuse to be put out.

Life was what it had always been in this small Texas town. Everyone had their issues, their dysfunctions, but most people got along and were there for one another when times were hard. Meals were delivered after babies and funerals, gossip spread at the local hair salon, eggs were borrowed by neighbors. The pastors of the handful of churches all knew one another and, for the most part, worked together for the common good of the people of Parkland. Theological differences did not matter one iota when a grandmother was on her deathbed or a child was ill. There was still a level of naïveté in Parkland, Texas, that would be ridiculed by some, envied by most. Parkland was a town where neighbors were still neighborly and most businesses were still closed on Sunday. It was a safe little town in which to raise a family and grow old.

Carl and Miranda argued quietly behind the door of their bedroom. The three younger girls sat in the living room in front of the TV. Tension was palpable in the air around them, and Carl shook his head, not wanting to listen to Miranda's concerns.

"She is too young. You should have waited longer."

"No, it's better now. She has to know what is expected of her early. It is safer that way long-term. If we had waited she might have acted out and given us away. She'll get used to it. They always do."

Miranda swallowed back fear. Rosie was refusing to eat today, lethargic and depressed. She knew the drill, had gone through this with all the girls—had been through it herself, though it had been so long ago that she couldn't remember the first time. But it got harder and harder to see the little ones suffer. She had to be careful with Carl because if she angered him he would exert his authority over her and force her to be silent. She had the makeup tricks down pat to cover bruises.

And she sure couldn't afford to be kicked out and left behind. With no documents proving her existence, getting a legitimate job and having an average life would be impossible.

And if she went to the authorities?

Ha.

Even if the chief of police hadn't been one of their patrons, Carl would find out and he would be sure she never spoke to anyone. Ever again.

She sighed in resignation and put on her steely face to go out and check on the girls. She worried about Hannah being gone for so long. What if . . . ?

But no, Hannah was smart. They had trained her well. Allowing her to go to the local school and have friends was a good cover and good currency to use to keep her in line. Hannah would do anything Carl asked at this point in order to stay in Parkland. She played the good girl like a pro.

Miranda went into the living room where the girls sat like zombies in front of the television. Carl had promised they could play outside today, but had not yet followed through. Now was as good a time as any.

"Why don't you three go outside for a few minutes? You can play in the garden."

Jessie's eyes snapped wide open and she jumped up, grabbing both of Rosie's hands. "Let's go, Ro-ro! Let's go outside!" Rosie stood up sleepily and followed her to the back door. Jessie opened it wide and the two of them stepped into the sunshine. They looked around for a moment, eyes blinking against the late morning light, trying to decide what to do next. Jessie spied a cluster of late-blooming pink roses near the concrete slab that served as a back porch and plucked one off, sticking it in Rosie's blonde hair and smiling.

"Let's play wedding!" Happily the girls picked flowers and took strands of English Ivy, weaving them into crowns and messy bouquets.

Miranda watched them through the window, glad to see Rosie smiling, and for a moment wishing this could be the norm. She went out to the front yard, realizing the flower beds, which had been so beautiful when they moved in, were becoming overgrown and full of weeds. The growing season here in Texas was much longer than it had been up north. She didn't have the first clue how to maintain a flower garden, but in the absence of anything better to do, she decided to give it a shot. She knelt down in the grass and pulled a spent dandelion out of the ground.

Then another, and another.

This felt good. Therapeutic. She looked with satisfaction at the dirt under her fingernails. A rare sight. Carl would not want her hands dirty or calloused, though.

She went into the kitchen and, since she didn't own any gardening tools, got a big metal spoon and a rusty pair of scissors. They would do for now. She made a mental note to buy basic gardening tools the next time she ran errands. Surely Carl wouldn't mind. He did want things to look normal, right? An out-of-control yard in this quaint little neighborhood would certainly look anything but normal. He didn't like anyone hanging out in the front yard for fear that neighbors would be tempted to stop by and visit, but a little weed pulling and hedge trimming during the quiet hours of the day surely wouldn't draw much attention.

AWAKENING

Violet walked across the lawn to her daughter's trailer, two eggs in hand. Nora met her at the door with a sheepish grin.

"Thanks, Mom."

"Well, of course! I'm so glad to see you cooking again. I'm sure those kids are, too. What has gotten into you?"

"I don't know." Nora took the eggs and walked through the dark living room, her mother following close behind. "I guess I finally just got tired of being mad. I have cried until I can't cry anymore, and the boys have been getting in trouble, and Kelley stays gone more and more." She shrugged. "My life has been spiraling down and I've been miserable. I hit bottom and looked up, realizing that I had two choices: live or die."

Violet silently thanked God for answered prayers. "I'm glad to hear that. I've been so worried about you."

"I know, and I'm sorry. I still have a lot of work to do, but I want to do it. I want to live. I don't want my husband to win any more. If he ever came back here, I want him to see that I didn't need him to be happy. I can do this by myself. He doesn't get to control me anymore from wherever he is."

"What brought on this epiphany?" Violet was shocked to hear the change in her daughter's outlook on life. This was a complete reversal.

"I talked to a lady at the church downtown, the one the Greens go to. Her name is Mrs. Miller. I ran into her at the store and she asked me how I was doing, that they had been praying for me in her women's class at church, and I just burst into tears. We ended up sitting outside the coffee shop next door for two hours while I spilled my guts. I was afraid she would think I was crazy, but she just listened and acted like she really cared about me. I don't know—something just changed inside me and I feel like I have hope for the future for the first time since he left." Nora looked at her mother through clear eyes.

"I need hope, Mom. More than ever, I need it."

Violet smiled at her daughter, placing her weathered hands on Nora's shoulders and peering hard into her face. "Then you hang on to it with white knuckles. Hang on no matter what this world throws at you. If you have hope, then you have everything you will ever need." Her voice was low and fierce, her eyes like flint. "Hope is like a light piercing the deepest darkness. Darkness doesn't stand a chance against it."

Nora smiled, tears stinging her eyes. She swallowed hard to keep them from spilling over. "I will. I promise."

Melody sat in history class, waiting for the bell to ring. Coach Hillman had finished his lecture and just a few minutes remained in the period. The kids were getting rowdy, and he reminded them to keep it down. Melody, though, was lost in thought.

She hadn't seen Hannah all week. It was Wednesday and Hannah had apparently been sick. Melody had tried to visit, but Hannah's father had met her at the door, telling her that Hannah wasn't feeling well and could not have visitors. He promised to tell Hannah that Melody had visited.

Thanksgiving break had come and gone. Melody's mother had tried to invite Hannah's family for dinner but, as usual, they declined ever so politely. Allie tried to understand, telling Melody that some people just aren't "neighbor people." True, Melody thought, but they never even seemed to walk out their front door. The school-aged girls were outside exactly long enough to catch the bus in the mornings and get off in the afternoons, and that was it. They never played out front or pulled back their curtains. Their family seemed so closed off. Hannah loved to come over to Melody's house, but she never, ever invited Melody over to hers. More than three months into the school year, and Melody didn't even know what Hannah's bedroom looked like. It just seemed weird.

The bell rang, breaking her thoughts, and Melody darted out the door and walked to her locker. She dialed in the combination and yanked the lock open.

"Melody!" Kelley ran at a full sprint to catch her before she slammed the door shut. "Hey Kel." Melody attempted a downcast smile for her best friend.

"Why so glum?"

"Just worried about Hannah. She must be really sick. Have you heard anything?" "Nope. I tried to call her but her mom said she can't talk because she's in bed. I feel so bad for her."

"I just hope she's okay. It's weird that we haven't been able to even talk to her on the phone, you know?"

"Yeah. I'm sure she's fine. Her parents just seem weirdly overprotective." Kelley shrugged. "I bet she will be back at school soon."

"Surely." Melody closed her locker. "So how was Thanksgiving? Did y'all eat at Granny V's?"

"Get this!" Kelley's eyes were huge. She leaned in closer for effect. "Granny V and Grandpa came to our house! My mother actually cooked Thanksgiving dinner!"

"For real? Dang! What has happened to her?"

"Sarah's Mom."

"Sarah Miller?"

"Yeah. Apparently she has been meeting with my mom on Wednesdays. I don't know what they talk about but my mom has totally changed. She is suddenly acting like . . . a mother again." Kelley smiled at Melody. "Everyone seems happier—except the boys. But they are idiots anyway."

Melody laughed. Kelley's teenage brothers definitely had a penchant for trouble, and the disappearance of their father from their lives had only added to their rebellion. Nora had obviously been about to pull out her hair in frustration over the summer.

"Well, at least your mom is handling things better."

"Way better," Kelley said. "I honestly can't believe how different she is. Mrs. Miller must be a miracle worker."

"I wonder what she has been saying to her?" Melody said. Kelley shrugged and both girls darted through their respective classroom doors before the tardy bell rang.

Steam drifted gracefully from the coffee mugs sitting on the table as the two women bowed their heads. Wendy Miller spoke to God in her soft voice, asking for wisdom, for grace, for guidance. Nora nodded, taking a deep breath and exhaling a whispered "amen" with Wendy. Two Bibles lay on the table next to their coffee mugs. One was clearly brand new. The other appeared worn and frayed, marked up with colorful highlights and countless notes in the margins. Wendy showed Nora how to find the index in the front, explaining how the sixty-six books were organized and who wrote them. Then they opened up to the book of John in the New Testament.

"This is always a good place to start," said Wendy. "It is like home base. If you understand who Jesus is, then everything else will fall into place eventually." She pointed to the beginning of the first chapter. "Read this to me, Nora."

"In the beginning was the Word." As she spoke, Nora's heart quickened. "And the Word was with God and the Word was God."

"Who is the writer talking about?" Wendy smiled at Nora, elated to watch her begin her journey, and beyond thrilled to have the privilege of walking with her.

"Jesus?"

"Yes! Exactly. Jesus is the Word—has always been in existence even before the beginning of time. Keep reading. See here? It says 'All things were made through him, and without him was not any thing made that was made. In him was life, and the life was the light of men.' Now look here: 'The light shines in the darkness, and the darkness has not overcome it.'" Wendy looked Nora in the eye. "What does this say to you? What does this mean . . . to you?"

"That Jesus is stronger than darkness?"

"Yes, that is right! He is stronger, and that is the reason you are finding hope, Nora. He has begun to shine his light in you and that darkness doesn't stand a chance. The Word—this book in front of you—holds the key to defeating the darkness. If you read it—let it penetrate your heart and your life—then you will have the tools to overcome anything the darkness tries to throw at you. I'll help you as much as you want. You are not in this alone by any stretch!"

Nora smiled, overcome at Wendy's generosity and genuine

love for her. How had this friendship materialized, seemingly out of nowhere? How were two women, so completely different from one another, sitting in a coffee shop with Bibles? It was crazy.

It was a gift.

Despite all that Nora had been through, the months of pity parties and self-hatred, she somehow could see that she had been given a merciful gift. She also knew, deep down, that tossing it aside to continue on the path she had been walking would be the end for her.

She looked back down at the book in front of her, reading ahead while Wendy explained the verses. She got to verse 12 and her heart leapt in her chest.

"But to all who did receive him, who believed in his name, he gave the right to become children of God." Children of God? This girl, who had been raised in a trailer park? This rejected, worn out, middle-aged mother, whose husband had discarded her like one of his dirty socks, was a child of God? It made no sense to her. But here it was, written in black and white. Wendy said this book was filled with truth from cover to cover.

Nora looked at Wendy. "So how do you know how to understand all of this? The Bible is huge."

"It is a long process of learning. You start with one thing, like I am showing you today. Start with Jesus. Then you build, one stone at a time, one day at a time, one lesson at a time. Your knowledge will grow and you will find yourself seeing the world through the lens of this book right here. So many things that seem muddled and senseless will come into focus as you understand more and more of who God is. You will never know it all, never fully understand everything, but time will prove that you are changing and that He is working in you every day to make you new."

Nora smiled at Wendy. Her voice broke as she whispered,

"Thank you."

Wendy's eyes filled with tears. "No, sweet Nora, thank you. Thank you for trusting me and for letting me introduce you to my Savior."

WASTING AWAY

Hannah held her belly and moaned. The throbbing would not let up. It had been four days since Carl had taken her to the clinic. They told him she would be sore for a day or two, but this was more than sore. This was a deep, growing pain that was spreading throughout her abdomen. She looked at the sunlight peeking from between the dark curtains, illuminating specks of dust and lint floating gracefully in the air. Suspended. Dancing.

Hannah felt a hot tear escape and crawl from the corner of her eye down to the pillow where it joined the others that had fallen during the night.

"I'm sorry," she whispered to the baby she would never know.

"You know teenagers these days," Carl had said dryly to the intake receptionist at the abortion clinic. Hannah didn't realize he had lied about her age and her name. The paperwork said she was fifteen. The intake receptionist barely looked at Hannah, so it apparently didn't strike her as odd that Hannah was small and obviously in the earlier stages of puberty.

"We are not prepared to raise another child. She just wants to take care of it, you know."

Hannah had sat, mute, on the blue office chair in the corner while he signed for her. She knew better than to argue, but inside she wanted to scream out that she was twelve. TWELVE. That no one she knew at school had been pregnant, that something was wrong, that her life was not normal.

For the first time, she realized her life was not normal.

She wanted out. She wanted to run. But she was paralyzed by fear and the nausea that had been the first sign of her pregnancy. Carl signed away the life of the human being that had begun to grow inside her and she was led down the hall, past two closed doors, past the soft weeping of a young woman on a gurney, to the room where the procedure took place. Where her baby had been brutally taken, the sounds of the suction machine still haunting her dreams.

It was Friday now, and she was feeling worse by the hour. Carl never even checked on her. Miranda seemed a little sympathetic, but didn't offer any comfort to speak of. The younger girls tried everything they could to help Hannah feel better, but the emotional torment with which Hannah wrestled was only the tip of what was appearing to be a growing iceberg.

Something was terribly wrong. Hannah could sense it. Her body was out of control. Fingers of pain coiled from her violated abdomen and tore through an ever-widening area of her torso.

Maybe she was dying.

For a while Hannah welcomed the thought. She entertained the possibility that she could escape this life and go to "a better place." But did that place even exist? And what about her sisters? What would happen to them?

She thought about Melody and Kelley. Did they miss her? Did they think it was odd that she had missed a whole week of school? Were they worried about her? Hannah turned over from her back to her side, curling up in the fetal position with her arms crossed tightly over her belly as she fought rising panic. She fixed her eyes on the stack of library books beside her bed on the nightstand. She wished she had the energy to read, to mentally escape the waves of pain and fear that were washing over her.

Suddenly she heard a knock on the front door, and voices. It was Melody! *Oh, Melody*, Hannah wanted to scream. *Help. Please help me.* She was too weak. Her voice refused to rise above a whisper. The pain. Oh, God, the pain.

God.

Was He even out there? Would He help her? If there was a God then why was she hurting like this? Where was He?

Melody, please. I need you. I need help. I'm dying.

How would she ever get help? Carl would never take her to a real hospital. He would never risk getting found out and losing the livelihood he had spent years to gain. She had no telephone in her room, no way to call for help.

The window. Could she possibly open it? She crawled out of bed and, on her hands and knees, crept across the room. With all the strength she could muster she pulled herself up using the doll house and reached for the window. It was locked, but the lock was rusty. She put both of her thumbs against the lock and felt it wiggle. It was slightly loose—just maybe . . .

She placed her body against the wall for support and pushed against the lock with all of her weight and felt it give. Yes. She pushed again, fighting to ignore the searing pain in her abdomen that was threatening to rip her in two. The lock turned just enough to free the sash, and Hannah, suddenly full of adrenaline, pushed the double-hung window up about three inches.

There was Melody, walking away. Hannah put her mouth to the opening and called her as loud as she could. A car drove by and Melody didn't hear her over the roar of the engine. Hannah tried again, taking a deep breath and willing her voice to carry.

"Melody! Help me!"

Melody took two more steps and stopped at the curb in front of Hannah's house. She looked both ways, then stole a glance back over her shoulder.

"MELODY!"

Loud. Yes, that one was loud. Melody heard her. She locked eyes with Hannah for one heartbeat, long enough to see the volumes of fear and pain in Hannah's eyes before Hannah quickly and quietly closed the window, dropped to the ground and crawled back to her bed before Carl or Miranda caught her. She had barely made it when Carl opened her door.

"What was that?" he demanded.

Hannah looked at him, defeated. Her face glistened with sweat, and tears were running freely down her face now.

"Please, something is wrong. Please get help. I think I am dying," she whispered.

He looked at her hard, his mouth forming a tight line. His eyes shifted, glanced at the window, and back again. He was calculating—weighing his options.

"I'll call Dr. Sanderson. He is a faithful client. Maybe he can give you something."

Hannah nodded, sickened. Dr. Sanderson. *Yeah, he will be a great help*, she thought sarcastically. He was one of the faithful ones, for sure.

Melody stood still for three heartbeats. Her eyes searched the bedroom window from where Hannah had weakly shouted her desperate plea. Hannah had slunk down, out of sight, and for a moment Melody wondered if she had imagined what had just happened. But she knew, in her heart, that she had not. She turned quickly, then willed herself to walk at a normal pace across her front yard, past the Mimosa tree, up the two concrete steps to the porch and through her front door.

Then she ran.

She ran down the hall, following the sound of her mother's voice on the telephone back in her parents' bedroom. Bursting through the door, her eyes took in the comforting sight of her mother sitting on the edge of the bed, telephone cradled between her shoulder and ear while she twirled the long, coiled cord in one hand and swirled a glass of soda with the other. Melody's eyes filled with tears, and a million thoughts swirled through her head at once.

Allie looked up when she heard the squeak of the door hinges and immediately registered the alarm on her daughter's face. She told the person on the other end of the line that she had to go and set the receiver on the cradle.

"What's wrong, honey?" Melody's lip quivered and she tried to speak, struggling to know how to start. She swallowed hard and blinked, trying to clear her head.

"Hannah. Mom, something's wrong with her. She needs help."

Allie tilted her head slightly, pursing her lips in confusion. "What do you mean? Is she still sick?"

"Yes . . . no . . . I think . . . I don't know. Mom, I don't know what's going on but I'm telling you we have got to do something."

Melody went on to tell her mother what she had seen and heard. Allie tried to take it in, tried to picture what had happened, but her mind was filled with questions. None of this made any sense at all. She tried to calm Melody down, to reassure her that Hannah would be fine, that she must have misunderstood what Hannah had said through the window, but the more she talked the more agitated Melody became.

Finally, Melody snapped and shouted, arms straight down by

her side and fists punctuating the air, "I am not imagining this! I'm telling you that Hannah is in bad trouble, and I'm afraid something horrible is going to happen to her if we don't do something!"

Allie had crossed the room until she was standing face to face with Melody. Now she took a step back. Melody had never shouted at her, not like this. There was a deep fear and urgency that she had never seen before in her daughter's face, and her instincts told her to listen.

"What do you want me to do?" Allie asked softly.

Tears poured down Melody's face now—matching streams converging below her chin, dripping onto the floor. Melody had no idea what to do, and she said so.

Allie thought for a moment, praying silently for direction. She looked out the window of her front door, at the dark house across the street that had once been so lit with life and joy. The yard was overgrown, curtains always drawn, even on the most beautiful of days. She never saw the little girls playing out front. In fact, she couldn't remember the last time she laid eyes on Hannah's younger sisters at all. They consistently spent their time inside and never came out to mingle with the neighborhood kids. Only Hannah was allowed that freedom. Now, Allie wondered why.

She shook her head, willing her imagination not to go crazy. Throwing up a quick prayer, she strode across the room to the phone hanging on the wall and picked it up before losing her nerve. She dialed Wendy Miller's number, hoping Wendy didn't think she had lost her mind.

"She has an infection."

Dr. Sanderson looked at Carl, eyes clouded with concern.

"Her abdomen is hard and she is running a fever. She needs to go to the hospital."

Carl tilted his head to the left incredulously, raising his right eyebrow and pursing his lips until they grew pale. "You know as well as I do that the hospital is not an option."

"You could take her to Dallas. It's far enough away that you won't be recognized, unless you have clients traveling from hospitals down there . . ." Dr. Sanderson felt the hard lump of guilt rise in his throat. He swallowed and took a deep breath, willing it away.

"We do have clients in Dallas. Several. But I don't think that is necessary. Can't you just give her something? An antibiotic?"

"I can get hold of antibiotics, certainly. But this is advancing quickly. She really needs IV antibiotics to battle something of this . . . caliber." The doctor looked at Hannah's flushed face and put a hand on her forehead. "Do you know how she got sick? This is unusual for a girl her age to have a stomach bug turn into something like this."

"She had apparently become pregnant, despite the pills. I took her to the women's clinic and they took care of it."

"An abortion . . ." Dr. Sanderson looked Carl in the eye, hoping to convey the gravity of this situation. "It is very possible that there is fetal tissue remaining in her uterus. An infection like this would quickly result and could be fatal if she doesn't have it removed. This is serious."

Carl felt anger rising up. He stood taller, determined to intimidate the doctor.

"All the more reason to get her started on antibiotics now. Bring in an IV if you must. We need to avoid hospitals if at all possible."

"I'm not sure it is possible. If she goes septic I don't have the equipment or expertise you will need to save her. I'm a family doctor, not an infectious disease specialist."

"Try."

There was no changing Carl's mind. Dr. Sanderson agreed to return with an IV and antibiotics by the end of the day.

Hannah drifted in and out of consciousness, hearing just enough to confirm what she had felt: she was dying. Fear was no longer causing her heart to race, though. Instead she felt a strange calm, like a hand was holding her still while waves crashed all around her. She let the world fade to black and sank into the peace that enveloped her.

FALLING SCALES

Wendy Miller stared absentmindedly out of the window of her study. It overlooked a small stand of white rosebushes that lay dormant. Her heart was racing, her stomach churning as she processed the disturbing phone call she had just received from Allie Green.

There had been talk among the city leaders about the suspicion of sex traffickers moving into the area, lured by the proximity of Parkland to larger towns and cities and by easy access to the interstates connecting metroplexes such as Dallas and Oklahoma City. News reports were circulating of trucks, crossing the border from Mexico, being seized. Border authorities had, on multiple occasions, discovered girls and young women hidden in the trailers. These girls were apparently being illegally transported for "work" in the United States. There had been stings in multiple cities where trafficking victims had been found locked in seedy motel rooms, and the reports had gotten closer and closer to the North Texas area.

Wendy knew in her heart that it was heading their way and had felt the prompting of God to get involved and be part of the solution, to identify the traffickers and organize rescues to free the young girls who were being enslaved. She searched headlines, scoured newspaper articles, contacted leaders of rescue organizations in other communities, and had begun the process of creating a network of watchful eyes in the North Texas area that could canvass the smaller communities along the interstate for signs of trafficking.

Allie's phone call had rattled her. Everything she had said raised red flags: young girls who were isolated from the surrounding neighborhood, parents who were secretive and reclusive, a child missing a long stretch of school with no explanation, the cry for help from the bedroom window. Wendy had asked Allie if there was a lot of traffic to and from the house and, at first, Allie had said no. But then, after thinking about it, she did say that she had noticed cars in the driveway late at night, especially on weekends. Other neighbors had mentioned parties as well, with several cars lined up the alley behind the house, but everyone had figured that the family was just entertaining friends. Often.

Alone, none of these things would have caused most people to suspect anything nefarious going on in the little white house on New Hope Lane. But when all of these small incidences were put together, Wendy felt she needed to investigate. Was it possible that trafficking had, indeed, arrived in this small town? Could Parkland be a new hiding place for such unspeakable evil —this quiet little town full of churches and beauty shops?

Wendy picked up the phone and dialed the number of the school principal. He was an important ally, knowing that his school often housed very troubled children. Maybe she could get his eyes focused on Hannah and intervene if at all possible.

Their conversation was short and to the point. He had, in fact, noticed that Hannah seemed troubled. She had two friends to his knowledge, Melody and Kelley, but otherwise kept to herself, spending her free time immersed in books. Of course, preteens were ripe for drama and angst so he didn't want to jump the gun and make unnecessary assumptions, but knowing what

Melody had seen alarmed him. He had dealt with abused kids before, and this situation was definitely putting him on high alert. He told Wendy he would make a phone call to Hannah's parents to check on her.

The ringing telephone startled Carl, who was deep in thought. Anger caused his heart to pick up speed, and he steeled himself, willing the frustration not to show in his voice when he answered. This situation with Hannah was a threat. He had to figure out a way to deal with her without bringing attention to himself or the girls.

"Hello." His voice was flat.

The friendly voice on the other end was not what he wanted to hear. It was the school principal, wanting to know if Hannah was okay. She had missed the entire week of school and he supposedly wanted to check and see if they needed anything.

Carl was seasoned. He could smell meddling a mile away. He assured the principal that Hannah had the flu. Yes, of course he had taken her to the doctor and they were advised to keep her home and let her rest. He wasn't sure when she would return to school but would certainly be sure she was not contagious before bringing her back. No, they didn't need anything. They had things under control.

The principal ended the conversation and put the phone on its cradle. He sat back in his desk chair and drummed his fingers as his mind turned over the few facts he knew, combined with the suspicions surrounding Hannah's family. Suddenly he stood up and yelled his wife's name.

"I need you to make your famous chicken noodle soup! Tonight!"

Carl saw the writing on the wall. It was as if unseen eyes were pointing lasers at him. The claustrophobic feeling was all too familiar, and he was beyond livid that it was forcing his hand so soon. They had barely been in Parkland for three months; he had never had to escape prying neighbors this quickly. Hannah's pregnancy and now this infection were ruining everything. He wondered how he might dispose of her without getting caught, but a plan like that would take time, and time was quickly running out. She would be dead before he could kill her, at the rate things were going. Where was that damn doctor, anyway? He needed that IV set up and soon: the girl was getting weaker by the minute. He could not afford to have her death questioned and everything he had worked for go up in smoke.

He cursed under his breath and strode into his bedroom where the computer sat on his desk in the corner. Pressing the power button, he waited as the machine hummed to life. Beside the screen with an orange cursor blinking against the black background, his modem buzzed and whirred. Carl began typing the cryptic message that would end his local business until he could relocate. Across town and as far as cities three hours away, his clients would be informed that services were being temporarily suspended. The dolls would be packed safely into storage and moved to a new location where they would once again be on display. When the toy store reopened they would be notified.

It was time to leave Parkland.

The principal's wife pressed the plastic lid firmly onto the orange Tupperware bowl, making sure the soup didn't have an opportunity to leak. She carried the container into the office where her husband sat, staring at a small stack of papers on his desk. He glanced up at her and smiled, thanking her for cooking the soup with such little notice and assuring her he would be careful when he paid his unannounced visit to Hannah's home.

He tucked the bowl under his arm and walked out to his car. Securing the soup between his briefcase and the back of the passenger seat, he pulled his seatbelt across his chest and buckled it before putting the key in the ignition and starting the car. As he backed out of the driveway he breathed a prayer for guidance. Never in a million years did he imagine, when he first told Wendy Miller that he would be involved in her child protection network, that he would actually be dealing with a situation like this.

He drove across town, noticing the bright gold edges of the clouds as the sun set in blazing glory. To think that a young girl like Hannah, who should be carefree and enjoying the typical life of a preteen, could be subjected to abuse of any kind raised every protective instinct he had as a man and a father.

Maybe he was wrong.

He told himself that he could be jumping to very wrong conclusions and that maybe he was just being hypervigilant. He prepared himself to see Hannah sitting on the sofa in her house, watching TV. Her father had said she had the flu. Though there had not been any cases of the flu at school yet this season, there was always the first and it usually lasted about a week. Yes, surely she was beginning to feel better by now.

He stopped at the red light marking the last intersection before turning into Hannah's neighborhood. His left blinker clicked its familiar rhythm. The sky in his rear view mirror exploded with red, gold, and pink. Sunbeams escaped from the edges of the clouds and fanned out across the heavens. The green arrow appeared and he turned into the neighborhood, driving slowly until he saw the sign for Newhope Lane, and turned right. His eyes scanned the numbers nailed to wooden posts topped with colorful and varied mailboxes for the house belonging to Hannah and her family.

There. There it was. Noticing the drawn curtains and mostly-neglected flower beds, he parked in the street and turned off the ignition. He watched the little house for signs of life but saw none. Reaching across to pick up the Tupperware container filled with warm soup, he opened the driver's side door. His left leg swung out and he stood next to the car, then walked up the concrete driveway, across the narrow sidewalk lined with leggy, faded chrysanthemums, and up the single step to the porch. The screen door hung just slightly off kilter, not quite securely latched. He quietly pulled it open just enough to rap on the wooden door.

One, two, three.

The sound seemed hollow.

He waited for several moments and raised his fist to knock again when he heard footsteps. The doorknob turned and rattled as whoever was on the other side of the door struggled to open it. At last it gave way and a little girl stuck her face into the slight opening she had created, staring fearfully at him.

"Hi there," he said softly. "Is your mommy or daddy home?" The little girl quickly closed the door. He heard her footsteps shuffle away and wasn't sure what to do next. He decided to knock again.

One and a-two and . . . three, four.

Voices. Hushed, scolding. He couldn't make out the words, only the tone of voice as a woman spoke to, he assumed, the little girl.

Should he knock again?

The door knob turned again, and this time a woman opened the door. She was incredibly beautiful, tall and striking in stature. She wore a lot of makeup that had apparently faded as the day wore on, and he noticed a dark discoloration on her right cheek. A fading bruise? Surely not. He mentally chastised himself for assuming the worst.

"May I help you?" The woman's voice sounded soft and husky. Her thick Spanish accent was captivating.

"Hello ma'am. I . . . I am Mr. Woodruff, the principal at Hannah's school. I spoke with your husband this afternoon and he said she's had the flu. I wanted to help, so I brought some of my wife's homemade chicken soup. This stuff will cure anything . . ." His voice trailed off as he laughed awkwardly, clearing his throat. Why was he suddenly nervous? He dealt with kids and parents all the time. But this was different for a reason he couldn't quite put his finger on. He forced a smile and held the soup container out as an offering, hoping she would take it.

She did.

"That is very kind of you, thank you."

He decided to take a big risk: "Would it be all right if I peek in on her and just say hi?" The woman's eyes darted back and forth.

"Uh . . . probably . . . she has been sleeping a lot. Probably not a good idea today. But tomorrow? Maybe you can come back tomorrow around lunch time?

His brow furrowed. That was odd.

"Okay . . . Yes, I will do that. Please tell Hannah I was here and that we hope she feels better soon."

"Thank you, sir. Thank you." The woman looked around again, as if she was being watched. Then she looked him square in the face. This time she spoke firmly. Her eyes locked with his. "Lunchtime. Tomorrow."

The door shut and he heard the sound of locks being secured. What in the world had just happened?

Mr. Woodruff drove home in silence, the wheels of his mind

turning and trying to put the puzzle pieces together. As he pulled into his driveway, he decided to make a call to Wendy Miller and fill her in. He felt the burn of deep anger surfacing as he realized his worst fears regarding Hannah might just be true.

Sprinting through his front door, he went straight to the kitchen and picked up the telephone. He searched through the Rolodex for Wendy's phone number and dialed, waiting impatiently for her to pick up on the other end.

The phone rang three times before Wendy made it across her living room to the yellow telephone on the end table beside the recliner and answered, cradling the receiver on her shoulder as she sat.

"Hello?"

"Mrs. Miller, it's Mr. Woodruff from the middle school. I just visited Hannah's home and I think we may need to intervene." He continued, filling her in on his visit and the odd exchange between himself and Hannah's mother.

TURNING

Miranda stood with her back against the closet door. She realized she was holding her breath and allowed herself to exhale. Tears stung her eyes as the air escaped her tight lips.

What was she thinking? What the hell was she doing? Did she suddenly have a death wish? *Querido Dios . . .*

But her mind flickered with images of Hannah. She knew the girl was dying. She had been told by Carl to leave her be, not to coddle her or try to help her. That he would handle it. Compassion welled up from deep in her gut despite every attempt to push it back. Things were spiraling out of control and she had to do something.

For the first time in her life, emerging through the cloud of fear and bondage, Miranda felt the dawning of hope.

But no, this is crazy. First of all, did she really think there was a way out? Was there a single person in this Bible-thumping, podunk town who would even begin to care about a house full of sex workers? If they knew what she and the girls did for a living they would certainly walk away in judgment. Rightfully so.

Sluts.

Hookers.

Worthless pieces of trash.

Even if they got out, even if Miranda and the children some-how escaped the vicious life Carl had bound them to, where would they go? No job, no proof of her existence—her life in Mexico before she was taken from her village and driven across the border in a hot, filthy semitrailer, then sold to Carl by the Coyotes as a young teenager a distant memory—Miranda's only "experience" was acting as "Mother" to these girls and pleasuring the men who snuck in their back door after the neighborhood was safely tucked in bed.

But Carl was turning on her. His anger and physical attacks were becoming more frequent. Despite the provocative dresses and carefully applied makeup, Miranda couldn't hide the fact that she was getting older, and the attention of the men who frequented their business was turning more and more toward the girls. She also knew the second she was no longer marketable she would likely be found in a ditch somewhere.

She could hear Carl's voice in her mind—seedy, raspy, and nauseating, his breath thick with cigarettes and sodas, greasy hair slicked back and eyes narrow as he perused her.

"Letting yourself go? You know you have to stay pretty, my dear. They like the pretty ones. The young ones. I see the gray and they will too. No man wants a grandmother."

She was only thirty-four, but had lived a hundred years of daily death. Compartmentalizing, Miranda was adept at shutting away all emotion and reason so she could be successful at her "work," knowing that to feel or allow herself to think about how utterly abnormal what she was doing appeared to the world around her would mean certain death. Brutal death. Merciless.

Oh, how she longed for mercy.

Just to breathe free for one day—even one hour.

She stepped into the hall and stared at Hannah's bedroom door, where the girl lay on the other side, unconscious in a pool of sweat.

"*Dios*, if you are up there . . . if you are real . . ."

Miranda shook her head, willing the plea away. But it came nonetheless. It came in a broken whisper, the last desperate cry of a forgotten soul.

"Help me. Help us. *Ayúdanos*."

Wendy Miller watched the steam from the freshly-poured coffee curl and twist until it disappeared into the cool air of her dining room. Her mind turned over the events of the past few weeks, so many puzzle pieces struggling to fit together and make a complete picture. She opened her leather-bound notebook and looked at the list she had made the day before, after her meeting with Nora—names of trusted friends as well as acquaintances who happened to also be people with authority and would be able and willing to help with a potential rescue: The sheriff. Pastor Pete. Mr. Woodruff. Her own husband, Grant, and his buddies from his Army days on the flag football team.

Whom should she involve? How many men did she think would be needed? Would the sheriff believe her and handle things? She uttered a prayer for wisdom. How would they do this? With less than twenty-four hours to prepare, they had to come up with a plan quickly.

Wendy took a sip, leaving a faint pink lipstick print on the edge of the white mug. She reached up and massaged her bottom lip with her right index finger, lost in thought. The crosses on her dining room wall caught her attention.

"Well, I guess you are the only one who knows how this is all going to play out, huh?" Wendy spoke to the wall, a focal point for her conversation with God. "How do we get these girls out of that house alive? How do we bring justice and see that awful man punished for what he has done? What if he runs? What if they are all gone by the time we get there tomorrow?

"I'll admit I am scared, Lord. You know I've been working toward this, doing what you have asked me to do, learning and building this network of people who are willing to fight this evil, but it's all been hypothetical until now—newspaper reports and TV specials, rumors and suspicions. I honestly didn't know if it would actually happen here, and I sure didn't expect to be planning a rescue this close to home."

Wendy's eyes spilled over with tears as she allowed herself to imagine the hell those little girls were living, using it as fuel for her resolve, fire for her passion to see this to the end. She took a deep breath and walked over to her rolltop desk, reaching for the phone tucked in the right corner just behind the tape dispenser and stapler. Picking it up, she dialed her husband's work number and waited for his secretary to answer.

After the third ring she picked up: "Camden and Associates; how may I help you?"

"Hi, Elizabeth, it's Wendy. Is Grant in his office? I need to speak with him."

"Yes ma'am, he is. One second and I'll ring you back."

"Thank you," Wendy said, hoping her voice sounded more relaxed than she felt.

Grant Miller heard the familiar beep of his intercom and then the sound of his secretary's voice letting him know his wife was on line one. He closed the legal file he had been perusing and picked up the receiver, punching the first lit button along the side of the base.

"Hi babe. What's up?"

"Grant, we need to talk. I need your advice about something."

Melody practically ran to Kelley's house, her breath coming in gasps, showing up as white mist in the quickly cooling air of dusk. She had heard her mother talking again to Mrs. Miller, realizing the suspicions that had apparently been growing among several people they knew, and needed to get away to process what was happening.

"I'm going to Kelley's," she had said, and ran out the front door before her mom could protest.

Police, local military veterans, Mr. Woodruff—all these names being thrown about as her mother hurriedly worked out details of what sounded like a rescue operation to get Hannah and her sisters out of their house. She knew she needed to trust her mom and keep quiet. She knew sharing what she had heard could ruin everything, and Hannah could . . .

Oh, dear God: Hannah could die.

The reality hit Melody hard and she choked back a sob. What in the world could possibly be wrong with her friend that could make her look so sick, so ghostly? Reaching the Collins' trailer, she slowed. Kelley was sitting on the half-rotted wooden steps leading up to the door and saw Melody from where she sat.

"What are you doing here? Melody, are you okay?" Kelley could see how red Melody's face appeared, could hear her breathing hard, and her eyes looked puffy like she had been crying.

"Mel? Hey, what's wrong?"

Melody could only shake her head and look wildly around, eyes fixing on trees, telephone poles, ramshackle trailers, anything but the face of her best friend.

"I . . . I can't tell you. Oh, Kelley, it's bad but I can't tell you. Not yet. But I need you to trust me, okay? It will all make sense tomorrow, but I just need to hang out here for a while."

UNCOILING

C arl stood in the middle of the bedroom, pacing wildly and gesturing maniacally as he barked orders at Miranda.

"Please," she begged. "We have only been here a couple of months. How would anyone be after us already? We have been so careful. There's no way . . ."

"It's that damn girl!" Carl tried to restrain his volume to avoid being heard by the neighbors. "If she hadn't gotten knocked up . . ." He swore, filth spewing forth as he blamed Hannah, blamed the doctor at the abortion clinic, and looked hard at Miranda.

"You are useless anymore." His words bit deep, shaking her to the core. "Look at you— old, wrinkled; that black bottled crap you put on your hair isn't fooling anyone any more. I don't know why I have kept you around for as long as I have. You cost more than you bring in."

Miranda tried not to show the panic rising in her throat. "But who would take care of the girls? At least I keep them maintained and coach them. If I was . . . gone . . . you would have a hard time keeping up this charade and marketing them to new clients. You know that."

Carl's black eyes narrowed into snakelike slits. Miranda despised that man. If only she had the strength to overpower him and run.

"We are going. As soon as you can get the necessities packed, you hear me? I want us on the road before dawn."

"But what about the school? You can't just leave and not wrap things up legally; they will come looking." She needed to buy time—just in case Principal Woodruff came back at noon. Maybe he would bring help.

"We will be long gone before they realize we have left town. I'm not taking the risk of alerting anyone to us leaving. I've got to get Hannah out of here before she . . ." His mouth pressed tightly, forming a hard line, and he cursed again.

"Before she dies? Before you have to dispose of a body? What about Dr. Sanderson? Where is the IV he was supposed to bring?" Miranda's fear was surfacing, and anger followed close behind.

"He got caught up while he was trying to bag up the stuff. Someone started asking questions. He was afraid to move forward and left the hospital without the supplies. It may be another day or so before he can get it to us—and I can't wait that long."

Miranda's mind swirled as she tried to formulate an alternative plan that would delay their leaving by at least a few hours. She had to give the principal of Hannah's school a chance to intervene. Deep inside, she had an unshakable hunch that her life depended on him.

The girls sat in the dark kitchen as Nora placed the teakettle over the low flame on the old stove. The rickety trailer house felt darker than normal, despite the little tree in the corner that boasted a single strand of multicolored Christmas lights and silver tinsel.

100

A storm was approaching and the winds howled through the cracks around the door and window frames. The small television perched atop a once-discarded end table flickered as the meteorologist pointed and gestured toward the red splotches on the weather map.

It was going to be a rough night.

Kelley had asked her mother for permission for Melody to sleep over. Surprised, because Kelley usually stayed at the Greens' house, she happily said yes. It made her heart swell to think that Melody felt comfortable enough to sleep over for the first time in . . . well, Nora couldn't actually remember the last time Melody had stayed at their place. She could also see that something was wrong with Melody. Her eyes were puffy from crying, but Nora didn't want to pry, so she thought of the little lessons in hospitality that she was picking up from Wendy Miller and offered to make a pot of tea.

The silence felt large. It acted as a megaphone for the building storm. Metallic clangs eerily penetrated the sound of strong winds, and the ghostly moans gave the girls the creeps.

"Turn up the volume, Kel," said Nora. Kelley got up and crossed the room to the TV, grasping the silver knob between her index finger and thumb and turning it to the right.

"If you are in Cleveland County, now is the time to find a safe place, especially those living in trailer-type homes or staying in RV's. This storm is very likely to produce a tornado, and you need to be in a shelter immediately. Find a central room in the house or run to the nearest underground cellar, but if you are in a trailer, do not—I repeat —do not stay where you are."

Nora jumped as the teakettle's whistle blew, piercing the air. She turned toward the stove to turn it off, determining to stay calm in front of the kids.

"Mama, what should we do?" Kelley whispered.

"I'm thinking, hon." Nora took a deep breath and closed her eyes. She whispered a plea to God, asking for help, for wisdom, for protection. Looking at the girls, she made a suggestion. "Why don't we drive up the road to the high school? They always open their basement during storms, and we should have time to get there. Melody, I'll call your mom real quick and let her know. They may want to join us there."

Melody nodded, her heart heavy, wondering what to do about Hannah.

Poor Hannah.

Quickly she brushed the tears away that immediately gathered and pooled in her swollen eyes. Nora picked up the phone receiver and dialed the Greens' phone number, quietly talking with Mrs. Green and assuring her that Melody was safe. After a few moments of back-and-forth decision making, it was agreed that both families would head to the high school. At least they would have plenty of company as they waited out the storm—much better than being cooped up in a bathroom or dank underground storm cellar. Nora was grateful that her parents were safe in a Dallas motel, her mother having an early morning doctor's appointment in the city the next day.

As the sky grew angry, the Collins and Green families, along with dozens of other families in the little town of Parkland, drove in a slow parade up the main street with one blinking light to the high school, standing proud against the flashing storm-lit sky. The rain had begun and the wind was blowing harder now, driving cold moisture beneath collars and soaking already-chilled feet, despite the occasional pair of rain boots. How was this spring weather happening now, at the beginning of the Christmas season? It had been unseasonably warm today, thus sparking the swirling clouds and huge thunderheads as a cold front barreled its way into town—apparently determined to set things right. But it was the wall cloud rising—a menacing green-hued force overshadowing the city—that caused everyone to run from their vehicles and dart into the safety of the school as tornado sirens began to sound.

Everyone carefully descended the stairs to the school's basement level, settling along the walls of the hall and catching their breath as the sounds outside grew louder. Someone turned on their portable radio, hoping to hear a weather update, but only music was playing. The sound was oddly inappropriate when all anyone wanted was to hear a weather update.

The bouncy, happy lyrics of a song performed by Janet Jackson were nothing short of annoying in this moment. When would the DJ or local meteorologist let them know what was going on out there?

The sirens throughout the town continued to blare their warning, and everyone huddled in groups, families clustered together and the eyes of children wide with fear as they sat. Waiting. Praying. Trying to remember to breathe. Then there was the odd beep of the weather alert:

The National Weather Service has issued a tornado warning for Cleveland County until 8:25 p.m. Residents of Parkland should take particular caution as circulation has been detected in the clouds on the northern side of town near Parkland High School. Current reports state a tornado has not touched ground, but there is a high likelihood that one will if conditions continue to deteriorate.

Gasps were heard all along the hall as parents held their children more closely.

Another weather alert sounded:

The National Weather Service is reporting a tornado on the ground in Parkland. Repeat, a tornado is on the ground. Take shelter now. It is moving at the rate of four miles per hour along highway 64, heading south and threatening multiple homes on the north side of town. Do not attempt to outrun this storm. Find a safe place where you are and take cover immediately.

A roar could be heard outside, like a passing train. Melody wept. She knew there was no way Hannah was in a shelter. Her mother reached out to her and pulled her close to her side, breathing into her daughter's hair and whispering where only she could hear.

"I know you are scared, baby. So am I. But I have to believe God will protect Hannah. We have to believe. Pray, baby. Pray with all of your heart." She kissed the top of Melody's head and tasted her own tears.

STORM

Miranda watched the storm roll in through the back window of the dining room. She stood with the drapes slightly parted, held aloft by her shaking hands. The radio speakers reverberated with the storm alerts, warning the residents of Parkland to take cover.

But where? Miranda knew there was no way to leave this house. Carl was in their bedroom, frantically trying to figure out the fastest way to get out of town with the girls without drawing attention to their exit. What if she just walked out the front door? The storm was growing louder by the minute. Would he notice? Rosie and Jessie were playing in the living room, blissfully unaware of the approaching danger. Did she dare to just open the door and go? Was she crazy? She allowed her imagination to wander for just a moment, envisioning herself drifting down the street, the wind whipping her long black hair about her face and body as the cyclone dipped down and lifted her up —up and away from the hell she had come to despise.

The hell she could no longer survive.

She looked at Jessie and Rosie, and her anger rose. Over the years Miranda had chosen to downplay any remorse she felt over the fate of the girls. Her life had been one of abuse since she was a child, leading her to trade her body for the security of having a roof over her head, allowing herself to be sold to stay alive.

She remembered well the day she climbed out of the back of the semitrailer after crossing the Mexican border. They had promised a better life—the American dream. It had sounded like heaven to her poverty-stricken preteen ears. Her parents both dead, Miranda had been desperate. The house where she had been born had weathered too many years of rain and wind, and the roof was caving in, threatening to collapse with the next big gust. Then the men came with their promises.

She had willingly climbed into that trailer. Even at the age of twelve, she knew it was risky and that something bad could happen to her. Still, she chose to trust, a decision she would regret for the rest of her life.

But these little girls? No one knew she had not birthed them. No one was aware that they had been sold into this life just like her. They came to her as babies, born to other sex workers and traded like baseball cards in exchange for cocaine, heroin, or whatever drug of choice their first mothers used to numb their pain. Miranda had fed them, diapered them, and raised them at arm's length. She knew Carl's intended purpose for these girls from the moment they arrived in their "family" and, for the sake of her own sanity, had viewed them as material goods. Miranda had never considered them to be her family, and certainly not her children.

Hannah's illness had sparked something in Miranda, though. Watching her suffer, with no one to even wipe the sweat from her brow or brush her wet hair off her face, brought back painful memories of herself weeping in the night, her body used and broken, missing her parents. Wishing for a kind touch or even a gentle voice to whisper that everything was going to be okay.

Lighting flashed, the instant thunder shaking the house, and the girls jumped up and huddled together, fear clouding their little faces. Miranda stood, frozen. Again, she looked out the door. Her decision was clear.

They had to get out of here. Now.

STRIKE

As the tornado snaked through the little town of Parkland, Texas, it was selective in its attack. A dip here, a swerve there—it acted like a giant fist pounding down one structure after another. Barns, sheds, even a couple of houses collapsed into piles of rubble. Debris flew; entire air conditioning units were sucked up into the cyclone and then tossed aside like discarded building blocks. It crossed the main road in front of the high school and slowly headed south, with its eye on New Hope Lane.

Miranda quietly approached Leslie, Jessie, and Rosie.

"We need to go, girls. I know a safe place." At their looks of alarm she put her index finger to her lips and said, "Shhhh. It's okay. Trust me. Just be very quiet and let's tiptoe outside. You can't make any noise, you hear me? Pretend you are little mice. Be very tiny and quiet. Can you do that?"

Jessie dared to speak. "What about Hannah?"

"We'll have to come back for her," Miranda lied. She knew there was no way they could come back. Hannah, unconscious and growing more ill by the hour—she would likely be dead within days. Carl would never allow her to be taken away, and if he caught them sneaking out he would kill them all and run. Oh, he was so vile and evil. Miranda couldn't save Hannah, but at least she could save Leslie, Jessie, and Rose.

Jessie nodded, looking skeptical but filled with enough fear to be willing to do whatever she was told to get away from the storm.

Miranda entertained the thought of calling Lucya but knew that was not a good idea. Lucya was so ingrained in this business, having been brought to the states from Russia when she was in her twenties and heading up her own lucrative brothel for years before connecting with Carl and retiring from active prostitution to head up his parties and network for business, she would probably warn Carl that the girls were leaving and stop the whole thing. Lucya lived four blocks away in a tiny duplex. Surely she was watching the news reports and hiding in her bathroom by now.

Miranda looked out the window of the living room, gasping at what she saw. In the not-too-far distance the funnel hung like a snake falling from the dark clouds. It writhed and twisted as it trudged through town. Up it went, then down again. Closer and closer it came.

It was heading directly toward them.

"Oh, God." Miranda sobbed. What were they going to do?

Carl heard the radio warning blaring again. He cursed and closed the briefcase on his desk. A well-crafted letter to the school, announcing the intention to withdraw Hannah and Leslie (due to his mother's sudden illness and their need to relocate to California to care for her, and would the school be so kind as to mail the transcripts directly to his P.O. box so he could share them with the school after he had them settled and enrolled in their new city?) was neatly folded and tucked into a stamped envelope to be picked up by the postman the next day. By the time anyone realized they had abandoned the house they would be long gone.

This out-of-season thunderstorm was a nuisance—or maybe it was the perfect cover. His mind spun as the idea formed and took shape. Yes, if they left in this mess, no one would even notice. Those nosy neighbors would never expect their entire family to leave in these conditions. Sure it was dangerous, but he was certain the odds of being hit by a tornado in December were much less than the odds of being caught and arrested at this point. He stormed out of the bedroom door and strode down the hall. There stood Miranda and the younger girls, appearing paralyzed.

"What?" Carl demanded. Miranda simply stood at the window, visibly shaking.

Then he heard the sound. The girls screamed as the air inside the house pressurized and their ears began to pop. Miranda leapt across the six feet separating her from the children and threw herself on top of them as the sound of splintering wood and breaking glass drowned out the rain and winds. The next thing Carl knew he was thrown against the wall behind the sofa and he landed on the cushions, disoriented and seething with anger.

"What the hell is going on?" he yelled. Miranda didn't answer. She lay on top of all three girls with them gathered in a heap beneath her outstretched arms and legs, determined to take whatever fell upon her own body, suddenly knowing her purpose in this moment was to protect them, even if it meant her own death.

Carl ran to the living room window and looked out as the tornado ascended into the dark clouds from which it had come. The room seemed to be intact except for the shattered window, so he stumbled down the hall to see where the damage had been done. The door from the first bedroom, where clients spent their thirty-minute slots with the girls, was hanging off the hinges. Shards of glass littered the floor and rainwater trickled in through the ceiling below the damaged roof. In the next room, miraculously, Hannah slept. She was so deeply unconscious that she had no awareness of what had just happened. The curtains covering her window flapped, revealing jagged shards hanging from the frame where the glass had shattered.

The air grew suddenly quiet. The storm was moving on and people began to emerge from their homes to assess the damage. Miranda stood, wiping blood from behind her ear where a flying piece of glass had nicked her, and the little girls lay still. Rosie looked up at her, tears running down her cheeks as she and Jessie sat up. Leslie covered her face with both hands and sobbed. Their confusion was evident as they tried to grasp what had just happened.

"You okay?" Miranda whispered. Jessie nodded and Rosie just stared at the window. Miranda opened the front door and tried to make heads or tails of what she saw.

Most of the houses appeared untouched. A few had obvious damage to their roofs, and the metal mailboxes that lined the street had been broken at their bases, hanging oddly askew, as what had been a mercifully-slender tornado had apparently tracked right down the center of New Hope Lane. Several telephone poles and lanky trees had been uprooted and lay on their sides, some blocking the road and forbidding any vehicle from coming or going. Sirens blared in the distance, but the emergency vehicles would be forced to stop at the end of New Hope Lane. Paramedics would have to be on foot as they canvassed the neighborhood to search for and, if necessary, assist the injured.

"Shit!" Carl's voice boomed from the hallway as he maniacally stomped into the living room. "We have to get out of here!"

Miranda hid the smile that threatened her lips—and her life. He was coming unraveled. In all the years she had lived with him she had never seen him like this. Of course, they had also never had to up and run overnight, either.

"It's okay, my love," she cooed. "Here, I'll help you gather everything so we can go as planned."

"Are you blind?" he growled. "How are we going to get down the street with those damn poles in the way?"

"It may delay us a little, but I imagine they will move them relatively quickly so the firetrucks can get into the neighborhood."

"Delay is not an option." His angry eyes bored holes into hers. "Delay will only land us in jail."

Miranda choked back a laugh, feeling suddenly emboldened. "Us? Why us?"

Carl glared at her. "You are a hooker, remember? You have been selling these girls—our daughters—and I just realized what you have been doing while I have been hard at work to support our family. Just wait until I tell the police!"

Miranda stared at him in disbelief. Was he serious? He was definitely delusional now. "What about Hannah? How are you going to explain her?"

He thought for a moment. "She got knocked up by a boy at school, and you lied about her age for her because she wanted an abortion. But you told me she had the flu and I believed you. I was so crazy about you that I never dreamed you would do something like this to our family."

Miranda realized that Carl was fully capable of convincing the police of this very story. The chief of police was one of their clients, after all. He had everyone he needed in his back pocket. Dammit. What little hope she had begun to feel escaped her soul and left her feeling more empty than ever.

She spoke more quietly this time, hoping for mercy. "We can still leave, Carl. Just lie low and give it a day or two. If the police come to our house we can tell them everyone is fine and they can move on. It's not like they are going to search our place or anything. They'll probably cancel school for a few days, and that will give us time to get everything together and leave without drawing attention to ourselves. I bet we could be out as soon as tomorrow night."

Carl stared holes into Miranda's eyes, looking for signs of manipulation or betrayal. But she was an expert at lying. He had taught her well. So Miranda held steady, appearing to be nothing less than loyal to her man.

Melody and Kelley were quiet in the car as they drove with Melody's parents back to their neighborhood in the wee hours of the morning. Nora followed them, assuming her already-rickety trailer was probably a casualty of the storm and allowing her younger children to go home with the Greens so she could assess the damage. She turned into the neighborhood a couple of streets before New Hope Lane and headed to her house. As the Greens neared the corner marking New Hope Lane they stopped, shocked by the trees and telephone poles blocking their path. Electricity sparked a warning from fallen high-line wires, and they dared not try to cross them on foot.

The Greens turned around and drove back one street, parking on Dover Drive and crossing through chain-link fences marking the backyards of neighbors to access their house which, by the apparent grace of God, seemed undamaged. Melody was anxious, so fearful for Hannah and wanting to check on her. But her mother counseled her to wait. The house across the street seemed to be only mildly damaged, so Melody took comfort in what her eyes could see.

As they entered through the back door, Allie picked up the phone receiver to see if it was working. Of course, the fallen poles had snapped telephone lines, preventing any signal from passing through, so there was no dial tone. She hung it up and sighed, knowing that wheels had been in motion to rescue Hannah and her sisters in just a few hours. She could only pray that the storm would not stop what had begun. And she could only hope Hannah wasn't so ill that she could not be saved.

TICK...

Principal Woodruff and Wendy Miller had been in the middle of a phone meeting, planning the details of an attempt to rescue the girls from what had clearly been revealed as a trafficking ring when the storm hit. Forced to take cover, their conversation had ended abruptly.

As the sun reached the far horizon, casting a bright orange glow and beginning its ascent into the morning sky, the citizens of Parkland began to clean up their yards and neighborhoods. Most of the damage had been limited to barns and sheds, but a handful of houses were badly harmed or destroyed. Debris littered many streets and yards.

Wendy Miller came out of her bathroom and looked around, thankful that her home was across town from where the tornado had touched down, and picked up her phone to try to reconnect with Mr. Woodruff. Unfortunately there was no dial tone. She uttered a prayer, hoping against hope that the plan they had loosely constructed could move forward. She determined to keep up her end of the deal, to have a social worker come with her, as well as written documentation of the evidence that had been being gathered by her, Mr. Woodruff, and the Green family.

Four police officers had been alerted and told to be in place by 11:30 that morning in unmarked vehicles. The plan had been to meet at the Greens' home, with the appearance of a luncheon or some sort of social gathering, in order to quickly and easily access Hannah's house and get the children out. There would be armed guards posted at each end of the street as well, in case they tried to bolt—or worse.

Wendy looked at the clock on the wall above her painted brick mantle: 8:30 a.m. Still three hours to go. She took a deep breath and sighed. With no way to communicate outside of her home, she had no choice but to sit and try to wait patiently. With every minute that passed, patience became harder and harder to come by. So much was at stake.

Principal Woodruff headed straight to the high school as soon as the storm was over. He knew there would be many families seeking shelter there and wanted to be sure everyone was safe. Sure enough, the people were emerging as he pulled into the parking lot. Some were holding hands; others walked alone. All wore similar dazed looks as the reality of what had hit their little town sank in. It could have been much, much worse, but still there was going to be a lot of work ahead of them to return Parkland to normal.

As the last citizens got into their cars and drove away, Mr. Woodruff and Mr. Caney, the high school principal, walked through all of the school hallways and checked every bathroom to make sure no one was still inside before locking the doors and walking to their own vehicles. They slapped backs and said goodbye.

The door slammed hard as Mr. Woodruff reached for his seatbelt and inserted the silver plate into the latch. He sat for a moment, gathering his thoughts. This was not what he had expected to be doing this morning. So many people who were supposed to help rescue those girls would now have their attention divided. How in the world would they be able to move forward after the town had been turned upside down? But he also knew Hannah was very sick and might not be able to wait much longer. He couldn't imagine what was wrong with her—what could possibly have taken her down like this—but from what Melody had told her mother, Hannah was obviously desperate for help. She had said Hannah looked like a ghost.

He turned the key in the ignition and the engine roared to life. He looked at the clock above the radio. It was 9:00 a.m. Two and a half hours to go.

Barry Gales, the youth pastor at Parkland Community Church, stood outside of the church's sanctuary atop the wide path of steps leading to the beautiful double oak doors of the main entrance. The huge Christmas wreaths that graced the tall doors hung in cheerful rebellion against the ugliness that had just struck the town. Barry had received a phone call shortly before the storm had passed through Parkland that had already troubled his very soul as the destructive winds began to blow.

He knew he had to be a part of this. Ministry could often be mundane, redundant, but not now. Not today.

To think that children were being held and used for—he shook his head and swallowed the lump in his throat. He knew Melody Green and her family well enough to believe what she had told her mother. Not only was it possible that her friend, Hannah's, life was in danger but it appeared there were more kids involved. Neighbors had reported seeing cars in the alley late at night, always assuming nothing, but when that fact was combined with what Mr. Woodruff had observed in Hannah's behavior, plus the other warning signs that had come to light, Barry had to trust that he had a part to play. This was a chance to shine light into the darkness.

Though he felt unqualified to handle children with such extreme abuse and trauma, he would step into it, hoping—trying to believe that God would orchestrate the details. Never in his short career would he have imagined being involved in something like this. A child sex ring? In Parkland? Things like that just didn't happen here. Who would even take part in such a thing? His mind reeled with possibilities and suspicions. Obviously there was demand or it wouldn't exist. It was beyond anything he could comprehend. Little girls—dear God, what kind of monster would want to hurt little girls?

He shook his head to clear the thoughts before they took hold of him and pulled him in an emotional downward spiral. He had to focus, to be prayerful in moving forward and find out what, if anything, he could do to help them—especially Hannah—if the police managed to get them out of that house safely. And of course he worried about the Greens. Being right across the street—what if the man holding the children tried to harm the Greens in retaliation?

Barry was relieved that the church was undamaged and prayed for the same grace for those little girls, then turned, opening the tall oak doors and walking though. As he closed the doors behind him, the bright evergreen green wreaths shook. He looked at the clock above the second set of doors separating the foyer from the sanctuary proper. It was ten o'clock. Only an hour and a half until he had to be at the Greens' home.

Nora wept as she stood before her broken trailer home. She looked across the yard to her parents' trailer, lying on its side. Thank God they had driven to Dallas the night before to see an orthopedist this morning about her mother's knee. With the phone lines down, she had no way to contact them and tell them what they were coming home to. Surely it was being reported on the television and radio stations.

Nora stood before the rubble that had once been her home. Memories flooded, along with her tears. Her five babies, the abuse she had survived at the hands of her husband, the aloneness she had lived with after he abandoned them—life in this house had been always hard, always dark. Only recently had she begun to experience hope as a result of her relationship with Wendy Miller, their weekly coffee dates, and her newfound faith in God.

So where was God now? How could He have allowed this to happen? It's the end of November, for crying out loud. November thunderstorms were not uncommon in this part of Texas, but November tornadoes were.

Her home was gone—reduced to a pile of splintered wood and twisted sheets of steel. She didn't even know where to start with sorting through the mess, much less cleaning it all up. And where would they go now? She had no money; her teenage boys had no jobs and wouldn't even fold their own socks, much less help with a huge job like this. She fell to her knees and wept. Hot tears rolled down her face as the pain of the last five years overtook her and she broke. Her cries escaped her lips, riding on the breeze, and a pair of cardinals flew from a low branch to higher footing, startled.

Nora let it all out—all of the grief, all of the pain, all of the anger. She pounded the ground with both fists, not even registering when they became bloody and raw. She shook those bloody fists at God and demanded an answer to why, when she finally thought life was going to get better, He would do this to her. Didn't He know she'd had all she could handle? Didn't He see how exhausted she always was? Did He not care? Was her life just a game? Was she just a pawn?

Finally Nora ran out of tears, at least for now. She stood on shaky legs, wiping her hands on her skirt and noticing the blood for the first time. Neighbors who had heard her weeping cautiously approached her, offering to help. Most of the houses surrounding hers were proper, sitting on firm foundations, and therefore survived the storm with very little visible damage. This freed the owners to come to her aid, moving Nora back into her weepy state. She had always kept to herself, avoiding the neighbors out of shame over her miserable life and living conditions. But now, she had no choice but to look them in the eyes, to meet their kindness with a nod and quiet "Yes. Please. I don't know where to start." And in that surrender, in that place of knowing she could no longer take one step forward alone, Nora was flooded by grace. Nora became known to those who stepped in to help her and was surrounded for the first time in her life by a caring community.

Her relationship with Jesus Christ had been only the first step. This moment, this leaning on the shoulders of her neighbors and not allowing shame to keep her locked up and alone was the beginning of her new life.

Hope was dawning.

As they began picking through the rubble of her old life, Nora paused to look at her wristwatch, taking a long, deep breath. Ten-thirty: plenty of time in the day to make a big dent in the mess.

Pete and Allie Green sat in their living room with Melody, Jake, Kelley, and Kelley's younger sisters Kristy and Mae. The kids were happy to be together, especially the younger ones who didn't fully grasp the gravity felt by the older kids and adults. Kelley, of course, had no idea what was weighing on the minds of the Green family, and Allie knew she would be very confused when police officers, social workers and pastors—not to mention Principal Woodruff— showed up at their house in just under an hour. The electricity was out, probably for a couple of days due to the fallen poles blocking the street. Thankfully the Greens had a gas grill on their back patio, which would serve them well for the next day or two, as long as the refrigerator/freezer stayed shut and kept the frozen meat from thawing. Pete decided he would venture out in a few hours to purchase a generator, which would keep their groceries from going bad until the electricity could be restored.

Allie asked if anyone was hungry, and all hands went up immediately. It had been a long morning, and no one had even thought about breakfast. She walked into the kitchen and quickly opened the fridge long enough to grab some ham, sliced American cheese, and mayonnaise. Grasping the bread bag by the gathered end, she picked it up and carried everything to the kitchen island where she put together a stack of simple ham sandwiches. Crossing the kitchen again, Allie took a bag of potato chips out of the top cabinet and found a few paper plates in a drawer. After assembling everyone's lunches, she brought them into the living room, two at a time, for once not caring if the kids ate on the living room furniture.

The sandwiches tasted like manna from heaven. They were devoured, along with the entire bag of chips, within a few short minutes. The room was unusually quiet as everyone ate, not only taking in the meal but also processing what the next days and weeks would hold: cleanup, repairs, and rebuilding for some.

Allie worried about Nora, knowing her dilapidated trailer house could in no way survive even a casual pass by a tornado. But without phone service, all she could do was pray and take care of Nora's younger children so their mother could take care of whatever needed to be done. She hoped Nora would come to their house and tell them everything was fine, but judging by the path of the tornado, Allie knew there was a strong likelihood that was not the case.

Allie glanced down at her watch. It was eleven o'clock. Everyone would be arriving soon . . . at least that is what she hoped.

One by one the cars arrived, parking on streets surrounding New Hope Lane: Mr. Woodruff, a social worker from the local Department of Children's Services, the sheriff (accompanied by two plainclothes officers), and Wendy Miller approached the Greens' home separately, subtly, not wanting to draw the attention of any of the neighbors, much less Hannah's family.

They had hoped to have the chief of police along as well, but he ended up occupied with the needs of the town as it began to clean up the debris from the previous night's storm. When the sheriff had informed him of their mission, he had suggested they wait a few days to get the bulk of the cleanup done. Wait? The sheriff couldn't believe the chief suggested that. Why allow those girls to suffer further abuse? There was no way that could be justified, tornado or no tornado. The chief tried to argue the point, but the sheriff quickly silenced him, letting him know the decision had been made and the plan would move forward.

So, as the team of rescuers assembled, the chief went into a quiet panic. His guilt rose up in a chokehold and he fought for steady breath as he picked up the telephone to call Carl and warn him of what was coming. But, of course, the telephone lines were down and there was no way to get hold of him. No way to preemptively protect his own name and reputation from what would surely be the end of his career and marriage. Not to mention the fact that he could end up in prison. He walked in circles around his office, heart racing, and tried to come up with a counterplan to what the sheriff had in mind. But the only way to do that was to go to Carl's house in person.

He had no choice.

Walking briskly, the chief flew through the double doors of the station and nearly ran to his car. He flung the door open and put the key in the ignition as he pulled the gear shift back into reverse and squealed out of his parking space, shifting forward and hitting the gas to peel out of the parking lot. Station employees who were nearby jumped, startled at the noise. They looked at one another and shook their collective heads, wondering what in the world was going on.

Barry Gales was the last to arrive at the Greens' house. The small group of men and women gathered together in the living room in a circle, hands clasped and heads bowed. Barry prayed, something that was a normal part of his life, but a prayer unlike anything he had ever said before. This was big. The battle ahead had the potential to be deadly, and they all knew it, though no one spoke that understanding aloud. Barry prayed for protection, for guidance, for justice. Wendy Miller nodded in agreement, uttering "Yes, Jesus" as he spoke. The sheriff, obviously uncomfortable with the religious display, looked up from beneath his brow and noted the expressions on the faces of the adults in the circle. He thought of his own daughter, just eight years old—the same age as one of the girls in that house who were ...

The sheriff swallowed hard as Barry said "Amen," and the others lifted their faces. Wendy and Allie wiped tears away that were quickly replaced by more. The two friends looked at each other and smiled, crossing the space between them and enfolding one another in a tight embrace. The social worker composed herself and adjusted the manila folder in her hands. Allie reached down to the coffee table and picked up the box of tissue, offering one to Wendy, who took it gratefully and dabbed at her eyes. Their emotions were clearly raw, and the realization of what was going on just across the street was more than their hearts could bear.

The sheriff turned and stood before his officers. He looked back and forth between them and sighed heavily before he spoke.

"We've gone over the plan. You know what to do. We don't know if Carl is armed, or if Miranda is going to lose her nerve and side with him. Hell, they could both have guns. Be ready, expect anything and, whatever you do, let's get those girls out of there and put that monster behind bars where he belongs." The officers nodded, placing their palms on the hilts of the guns at their belts, hidden beneath the blazers they wore over plaid button-down shirts and blue jeans. Principal Woodruff approached the officers, asking what he needed to do.

"You are going to knock on their door just like you have before. Tell them you are there to help, that you noticed the damage to their house. Ask to see Hannah. We will be in position behind the shrubs near the front and back doors."

"They won't let me in, I know that, so what do I do when they refuse?" asked Mr. Woodruff.

"Well, let's see who answers the door. If it's Miranda, I'm hoping she will trust you and come out. If not—if Carl answers, then insist that you are there to help and can't, in good conscience, leave knowing Hannah has been sick all week. Whatever you do keep your eyes on them. Do not shift them toward us. It is imperative that you act like you are alone."

"Okay. I get it. Okay." Mr. Woodruff looked around the room. He took a deep breath and loudly exhaled: "Let's do this."

The chief arrived at New Hope Lane in record time, banging his fist on the steering wheel when he realized the street was blocked and that he would have to park elsewhere and walk. He drove on to the next street and turned, hoping to find a spot easily accessible to Carl's house— preferably to the backyard. Slowly he coasted down Caruthers Drive, setting his face like stone and focusing on the task at hand: his own self-preservation.

How had he gotten himself into this? His lust for sex, his addiction to pornography and the desire for younger and younger girls had grown and taken over every waking thought. His wife accused him of drinking too much, and he always made excuses for his distracted behavior at home and his lack of desire for his wife of thirty years. She blamed herself, thinking maybe she had put on too much weight or that her fading youth had made her no longer beautiful in his eyes. But the ugly, evil truth was that his affections, his obsessive pursuit of darker and darker experiences, had overtaken him and he was no longer attracted to any grown woman. He lusted after youthful innocence, greedily robbing it over and over from young girls like the ones Carl sold.

He got out of his car, crossing through yards and the muddy alley to access the back gate of the chain-link fence surrounding Carl and Miranda's yard. He slogged through puddles, not caring that his work shoes were soaked through, and tromped up the back steps to the screen door. He opened it and rapped on the wooden door that was most likely locked, the one that accessed the kitchen from the back porch. No one answered.

Muttering under his breath, he knocked again—louder and more firmly this time: One. Two. Three.

Footsteps. Voices. Still no one answered.

He cursed, angry at Carl's ignorance and becoming desperate to get in. He tried the handle and was shocked when it turned. Grasping the knob firmly, he turned it slowly, all the way to the right, until he felt the latch give way and he could push it ever so slightly open. He leaned in, putting one eye to the space he had created and looking to see if anyone was in the kitchen.

There, at the sink, was Miranda. She was bent over the basin full of dirty dishes, her long hair hiding her face. Her back rose and fell heavily, suggesting she was either out of breath or crying. He could not be certain. He knocked again, not wanting to startle her. She stood up straighter and turned, looking back over her left shoulder and spotting his half-face through the open door. She threw her hands over her mouth and gasped in fear, stifling a scream.

The chief quickly opened the door the rest of the way and held his hands up, saying quietly, "It's just me! It's okay . . . I . . . I'm here to help. Y'all need to go now. People know, and . . ."

"Know what?" Carl strode into the room with fury in his eyes. "*Know what, John?*" He stood nose to nose with the chief, anger filling the room and tension thickening the air.

"Somehow word has gotten out and—aw, dammit, Carl I'm just trying to help you! I don't want you to get caught any more than you do. You know how much I have to lose! Y'all need to go, and now. I have done everything I can to stop them without blowing my own cover, but their plan is moving forward and I can't do anything about it. Just get your stuff and go!"

Miranda exercised every ounce of self-control that she could muster as the reality of his words sunk in. Fear mingled with hope. Her hands began to shake and she looked at Carl, trying with all of her might to appear unflustered.

"What do you want us to do?" she asked.

Carl stood in disbelief for about three seconds and glared at the chief. "I want you to grab the girls and walk out that back door."

"But . . . darling, how will we get out of town? Our car is blocked," she gently reminded him.

"I'll call Dr. Sanderson to come pick us up."

"The phones are down," the chief reminded him.

Carl paused, looking the chief in the eye. "Then you will drive us out of town."

TOCK

Mr. Woodruff waited behind the Greens' closed front door as the sheriff and his officers went out the back door and quietly approached the house across the street. The sheriff and one officer positioned themselves behind the laurels, flanking both sides of the front door, while the second officer crept across the grass and around the side of the house through the front gate to hide behind another overgrown shrub, just a few feet from the back porch and underneath a window.

Mr. Woodruff could barely see the sheriff from his position and waited for the signal to go.

After about five tense minutes, a hand stuck out from behind the bush with a thumbs-up. "God be with you," said Wendy from just behind him.

"Uh . . . thank you. You too," he said awkwardly. She nodded and encouraged him to start walking.

One, two, three, four. He counted his steps as he crossed the wet asphalt and stepped onto the walkway leading to the front door. His heart was pounding in his ears. Across the street, Allie and Wendy held each other and watched through the small window, high in the closed front door. Melody and Jake had been told to stay in Jake's room with Kelley and her siblings, no matter what they heard. Pete was standing guard at Jake's closed door with a baseball bat in hand. Melody obviously knew what was about to happen, but Kelley and Jake were told that someone in the house across the way was sick and the police were there to help get them out because of the storm.

Mr. Woodruff approached the door and knocked twice. He could hear scuffling, voices raised and quickly hushed. Surely they didn't know what was going on. There was no way . . .

He knocked again.

Inside, Carl had snapped into action and was barking orders at the girls.

"Line up at the back door, now! Follow your mother out the back and do not say a word!" "What about Hannah?" Jessie asked, worried about her sister.

"She stays."

"But she's *sick*, Papa! Please don't leave her!" Jessie's voice broke and tears filled her eyes. Carl ignored her plea.

"Shut up, do you hear me? *Shut up.* We are leaving now." His voice was steel, cold and threatening. He knew that the discovery of Hannah would be a huge setback but, by the time she was found, he planned to be long gone down any of the various interstates running through North Texas. He could easily disappear again and reemerge a few weeks later in a new town with a new name . . . and a new business. His tone silenced Jessie and she quieted, her quivering bottom lip the only giveaway to her breaking heart. Rosie moved in close to Jessie, her thumb in her mouth and blue eyes huge. Jessie put her arm around her sister and stood, waiting.

Mr. Woodruff waited another minute, wondering what to do. He cast a sideways glance at the sheriff, who motioned for him to knock louder, which he did. One, two, three, four, five.

This time Miranda heard the knock and her heart skipped a beat. She looked at Carl, fear in her eyes, though this time the fear was not of the person at the door but of the man who stood before her—a man who had robbed her of life, of joy, and of any shred of innocence she had still possessed when he bought her.

"Someone's knocking," she whispered.

"Answer it," Carl said. He reached behind him and pulled out the handgun he had tucked into the waistband of his pressed black trousers. "I'm ready."

Violet and Joe's old Toyota Corona bounced along Highway 287 as they neared the exit that would take them to Parkland. It had been about an hour since Violet had turned on the radio, just after finishing the magazine article she had been reading and tucking it into the glove compartment. The news of the tornado that had struck Parkland early that morning came across the airwaves, sending shock and fear through their hearts and causing them to wonder what they would find when they arrived home.

If they had a home.

As they took the exit and turned back under the overpass onto the access road, the high school stood untouched in the distance. Violet prayed under her breath, hoping with all that was in her that it was a sign meaning things weren't so bad in their little town. They turned right at the second stop sign and crossed the railroad tracks. Up ahead were the first evidences of the damage done by the storm. A power line leaned dangerously over the street, tree branches littering the adjacent yards. Joe grunted as he muscled the wheel around to turn left onto their street.

"Looks bad."

Violet took a deep, ragged breath.

"Yes, it does."

Joe drove slowly, approaching where their mobile home had stood in disbelief. Violet's eyes struggled to take it all in.

Their home was lying on its side and Nora's was gone. A sob filled her throat and she cried out in anguish. Where was Nora? What had happened to her daughter and grandchildren? Joe put the car in park and got out slowly, his old bones protesting after two hours of driving. He walked around to the passenger side and opened Violet's door. She looked up at him, tears filling her eyes.

"Joseph?"

"Come on out, honey. Let's see what's going on." He took Violet's hand and elbow, lifting her gently as she moved her right leg over the threshold of the car and onto the muddy ground. She stood slowly, straightening her road-weary back to face the scene before her.

It looked like a war zone.

Together they navigated the treacherous ground toward what had once been Nora's house. Violet called Nora's name softly, then louder. Panic threatened and her throat tightened. She looked up at her husband of forty-five years and their life together flashed through her mind in a matter of seconds.

Their home may have been dilapidated and poor, but they had lived in it for more than twenty years, and it was all they had. Photos, knickknacks, and memories of happier days all were tied to that rusty green trailer with dark paneled walls and brown carpet. Violet's concern about their few possessions was completely overshadowed, though, by fear for their daughter and grandchildren.

Where is Nora? The question screamed through Violet's mind and she called her daughter's name as loud as she could this time.

"Mama? Dad?"

Violet's grip on Joe's big, weathered hand tightened involuntarily as her daughter's voice sang like a harp through the confused fog of her mind.

"Mama—over here!"

Violet and Joe turned around to see Nora approaching them from a neighbor's yard. Nora broke into a run and stopped just short of her parents, taking in the comforting sight of them before allowing them both to enfold her in their arms.

"Where are the kids?" Joe asked gruffly, trying to hold his emotions in check.

"The boys are with friends; Kelley is at the Greens' house with Mae and Kristy." Nora paused, looking back and forth at the tired, concerned eyes of her mother and father. "I'm so glad you are here. I'm so glad you were gone earlier, though." She looked at what was left of her parents' house and back at them. "You could have been killed."

The reality of what they had missed while in Dallas hit Violet hard, and she looked up at her husband.

"You're right. Thank the Lord we were away from all of this. But how did you . . . survive it? Your house, baby. It's gone."

"I drove with the Greens to the high school, along with a lot of other people in town. We all waited it out in the basement. When we realized it had hit this part of town directly, the kids split up with friends so I could come here and figure out what to do now."

Violet looked at her daughter, amazed at the level of calm she exhibited when faced with the loss of everything she had ever owned. She smiled at her, knowing from where Nora was drawing her strength, and feelings of sheer gratitude welled up within her, making her chest ache with fullness and joy in the midst of this very hard day.

"What are you gonna do?"

"I don't know yet. But for now the Carsons have said I can spend the night with them. I guess I'll start there and pray for direction. That's all I can do right now. I'm sure the kids will want to stay with their friends until I find somewhere for us to rent." Nora took a deep, shuddering breath, betraying the on-slaught of tears she had endured just an hour earlier. "I'll see if you can stay with me at the Carsons', okay? They have an extra bedroom and I can sleep on the couch so you and Dad can have the bed."

Violet started to protest but stopped, realizing arguing would be a waste of time right now. Instead she nodded, allow-ing her daughter to take the lead.

GO.

Mr. Woodruff held his breath, his mind racing as he prepared for what was about to happen next while having no idea what that would be.

Suddenly the doorknob turned and Miranda gingerly peeked out from the narrow opening, her eyes wide with fear.

"Go," she mouthed soundlessly.

"What?" Mr. Woodruff mouthed back instinctively.

"Go." Her teeth were clenched and her eyes bored into his. He inhaled and slowly shook his head.

"Hello Mrs.—uh—Mrs. Ruiz. I was just wanting to check on you, to be sure you're not hurt."

"Please go." She mouthed again, and motioned behind her with her head and side-cast eyes, but he shook his head slowly, lips pressed together in determination.

"May I check on Hannah? I know she has been sick for several days, and I'm concerned about her." He was grasping at straws, not understanding what was going on behind Miranda. She was very obviously afraid. He had no idea that behind her was a flurry of activity as the chief herded the girls to the back door in order to quickly escort them to his car where they, along with Carl, could be whisked out of Parkland.

The chief carefully opened the wooden door, holding it back with his hip as he reached down to unsnap the holster and grip his gun. With the other hand he turned the latch and slowly opened the glass door to the backyard.

"Come on," he growled at the frightened girls who were huddled together, tears streaming down their cheeks. He gripped Rosie by the sleeve of her pajamas and pulled her into position in front of him, causing the other girls to follow. They had only taken two steps beyond the threshold when an officer stepped in front of them, gun raised and ready, from where he had crept behind the open door.

"Freeze!" The word trailed off as the shock registered on the officer's face. "Chief? What the . . . ? What are you doing here?"

The chief thought quickly as he realized what was happening. "I, uh, was getting these girls outta here. What took you so long?"

The officer lowered his gun and looked at the girls, registering their fear. Leslie looked at him, back at the chief, then locked her eyes on the officer's. Mustering every bit of courage she had, she shouted, "He's lying! He's stealing us!" Then, in a whirl of motion she stomped on the chief's foot and pulled her sisters away from him as the officer raised his gun again and eyed the chief angrily.

"You nasty sonofabitch. You're in on this? You using little girls? Gettin' your jollies?" He stepped closer, aiming the gun right between the chief's angry eyes.

"Put the gun down, Ray."

"Not a chance, sir."

"I said, put—the—gun—down, Ray." The chief slowly began to lift his own gun from his holster.

PAPER DOLLS

"If I were you, sir, I'd leave that gun right where it is. One move and I will blow your perverted brains out right here in front of these girls. I reckon it wouldn't bother them one bit to see you dead." He cocked the gun and pressed it into the chief's forehead to make his point. Ray glanced at Leslie.

"Run. Hide. We'll find you. Just go to a neighbor or something."

In the moment that Ray looked away, the chief quickly pulled his gun up and aimed it at Ray, matching his stance and daring him to fire. Leslie grabbed Rosie and Jessie each by an arm, and they took off in a full sprint through the back gate and down the alley.

"You think you know what's going on, huh?" The chief's face was red with rage. "You think you got me? You thought wrong. I'm not going down for this. You want the guilty snake behind it all? Go in there and take down Carl Ruiz. Shooting me will only give him a chance to run while all hell breaks loose. Think about it, man. I'm not who y'all came after, and you know it."

Ray's head spun as he tried to make sense of what the chief was saying. Sure, this looked bad, but maybe he was right. Maybe Carl was the big fish that needed frying.

Back in the house Carl had stopped his attempted exit and stood, hidden, to the side as Miranda talked to Mr. Woodruff through the partially-opened front door.

"Hello Mr. Woodruff. Oh, I can assure you we are just fine."

"Well, that's good, ma'am. I . . . uh . . . well, can I see her? Just check in on her? I noticed the damage to the house and . . ."

"Oh no, really, she is unharmed. We were just leaving . . ." She glanced over at Carl, just two feet to her left and glowering at her. "Um . . . we were going to stay with some friends until repair can be arranged." She widened her eyes and jerked her head ever so slightly toward where Carl was hidden. Carl saw it and caught onto the signals she was sending. He pulled the hammer back on the gun and Miranda heard the click. Her eyes widened, alerting Mr. Woodruff that something was happening beyond his line of sight.

Mr. Woodruff took a step forward and put a hand on the door, slowly pushing it farther open and revealing Carl standing at the ready, gun in hand and cocked.

"He has a gun!" the principal shouted.

"BOOM!"

Carl fired the gun and Mr. Woodruff flew backwards, falling to the ground, bleeding from his right shoulder. His head hit the concrete and he quickly went unconscious while gunfire exploded all around him. As the world faded to black, he heard the sound of Miranda screaming and smelled the bitter iron smell of gun smoke.

Ray and the chief heard the gun go off and reacted in two different extremes. Ray ran past the chief into the house, while the chief sprinted to his car, determined to save face and somehow escape what was beginning to appear inevitable: the end of his life as he knew it, the end of his career, and the destruction of his reputation. This was bad and getting worse by the second.

Ray ran across the dining room and turned left down the hall into the front room where Miranda was screaming and Carl stood against the far wall, pinned in place by an armed officer, with his hands up and his gun lying on the ground. He was bleeding from a cut on his head just above the left temple, and the red streaks were making their way down his face, mingling with sweat. Miranda was on the floor, kneeling with her hands protecting her head as the noise died down.

"We got 'im, Ray! We got 'im! Go check on the sheriff out front!" Ray nodded and rushed through the front door, now hanging askew from being flung open by the officer and sheriff as they had rushed into the house at the sound of gunfire. Upon seeing Carl disarmed, the sheriff had bolted back out front, kneeling over the principal of the high school. Blood was pooling around the fallen man, and the sheriff was on his radio, calling for paramedics.

"It's all right, sir. You are hurt, but it's just your shoulder. I'm going to tie this handkerchief here tight to slow the bleeding, okay? Just hold on. Help is coming." He worked quickly as he spoke, looping the cloth over and under the principal's shoulder and tying it as tightly as he could. There was so much blood. He had to slow it down or . . .

Soon, sirens wailed and stopped behind the Ruiz's house. Shortly after, two paramedics appeared through the door, having parked the ambulance in the alley and run through the house to get to them because the street was still blocked in the aftermath of the tornado. They paused for a moment when they saw Carl and the blood on his face, but the officers urged them to keep going and tend to the wounded man outside.

They immediately set to work, attempting to stop the bleeding and assessing Mr. Woodruff's injuries. He was in and out of consciousness. A third paramedic appeared with a backboard and they carefully strapped the large man onto it so they could carry him safely. They started IV fluids and hurried back through the house to the waiting ambulance, where they turned on the sirens and raced to the emergency room in nearby Weldon. The sheriff stood up and watched as they carried the principal away, hoping—maybe even praying—that he would survive his injuries. He didn't deserve to die. He had put himself at great risk to help those girls.

The girls.

The sheriff suddenly remembered what he had been told about the oldest girl, Hannah. Where was she? Radioing for more medical assistance, he ran past Carl as he was being handcuffed, then down the dark hallway to the last bedroom on the left, the only room with a closed door. He tried the handle and it turned easily. Stepping into the room he saw her immediately.

Oh, dear God.

She was gray. Hair stuck in tangled masses where it had soaked in sweat across her forehead. She was lying on her side facing the door, and her eyes were closed. Thin arms were across her stomach, and she seemed frozen in time.

They were too late.

The sheriff sat carefully on the bed next to her, reaching out to feel her neck for a pulse. It was faint, but she was, in fact, alive.

He felt her forehead, so cold and clammy, and her closed eyes fluttered. Breaths came slowly and were shallow. How long had she been lying here, wasting away, alone? Anger threatened his calm, and he forced it back for now. All he could do at this moment was wait and pray the paramedics could get to her quickly.

Within a few minutes the second ambulance arrived. Two paramedics raced through the house with medical bags in hand and began to assess the sleeping girl. Things did not look good. She had an infection of some sort and it appeared she was septic. One of the paramedics ran down the hall to the living room. He asked if anyone knew what was wrong with her, and Miranda looked up from her crouched position and whispered the terrible truth.

"She had an abortion that went bad."

The paramedics looked at each other as their faces tightened in resolve. The odds were stacked against the sick girl, but they would do whatever they could to save her. They started IV fluids and antibiotics before placing her on a stretcher and rolling it out the back door, across the yard, to the ambulance parked just outside the gate. Once again, sirens screamed as Hannah was rushed to Weldon where doctors waited, ready to fight for her life.

The sheriff took a deep breath and sighed, walking down the hall back to where Carl stood, handcuffed, his face a smeared and bloody mess. Miranda had risen from her crouched position and stood, unafraid, for the first time in her adult life. She walked up to Carl, her rage barely in check, and spat in his face. He flinched and turned away.

"You lose."

Carl looked at her again, indignant.

"You lose, darling. It's over." Miranda ran her fingers through her long, black hair, releasing the ends from her outstretched right arm before placing her palm on his bloody cheek. "I have worked for you, served you, defended you, and watched you torture little girls for as long as I can remember. You broke me. I have nothing. I *am* nothing."

Carl smirked, relishing her admission. She had no life without him, she knew that.

"But today, I am someone. I am a woman who said 'enough.' I am a woman who would rather die than live the hell you have put me through one more day.

"You lose."

She leaned in close, her lips barely brushing his cheek as she whispered into his ear quietly enough that only he heard her: *"Y me asegurar é de que todo el mundo sepa todo."* (And I'm going to make sure everyone knows everything.)

With that, she stepped away and looked at the police officers with fire in her eyes. Carl sputtered in fury but did not speak.

"I will tell you everything you need to know. I have nothing to hide." Miranda held out her wrists and allowed herself to be handcuffed. She had, after all, been complicit in the sale of the girls to client after client, year after year. They would have to take her in and figure out what to do with her. And she would not resist.

Surrender felt so good. Though bound, Miranda had never felt more free.

Across the street, Allie and the others all stood just outside the Greens' front door, hands over their mouths and varying expressions of fear and disbelief on their faces. Things had literally blown up before their very eyes, and they still didn't know exactly what was going on over there.

Then, from the right, came the little girls who had been sent away by Officer Ray just before the shooting had begun. They were walking at first, obviously disoriented and confused, then broke out into a run when they saw the group gathered outside the Greens' house.

"Help! Help us!" they each cried. "That man was trying to steal us!"

"Which man?" Allie asked.

"The police man! He tried to steal us!"

"Who? Where?" Allie didn't know what they were talking about. "Were you over there, in that house?" She pointed at the house across the street.

"That's our house. The police man tried to steal us but the other one stopped him. He told us to run!"

"Okay, stay with me and we will figure out what's going on. You're safe here, all right? No one is going to hurt you." The girls nodded, huddling close together as Allie brought them into her house, where a surprised Wendy Miller was waiting with the social worker. Though she had never actually met these girls, only Hannah, she immediately realized exactly who they were. These children would need assistance far beyond what she could give them after what they had survived. She looked at the social worker: "You're up."

The social worker knew exactly what to do. She knelt down and introduced herself, speaking softly with the girls. Smiling, she gently and carefully began the process of gaining their trust if at all possible, assuring them that she was there to help.

Miranda and Carl were escorted, handcuffed, out the back door and into two separate police cruisers. Miranda cooperated fully, obviously relieved to be separated from Carl. Carl walked slowly, not hiding his rage, and muttering curses and threats with every step. The officer who had captured him held an arm to prevent him from trying to run. As they reached the car and opened the door, Ray approached them from behind.

"Hey, stop for a second," he said tersely. The officer did so and looked back at him, wondering what he wanted.

Ray looked at Carl, seeming to measure his height with his eyes. He closed the distance between himself and Carl, staring the bound man down and searching for words.

"You're a pimp? For little girls? You selling sex to the highest bidder? With *kids*?"

With every word Ray's tone grew harsher, his face red with righteous anger and his fists balled at his side.

"Well? Am I right?"

Carl smiled, pure evil rising like a vapor on his breath. He spoke clearly for the first time since being handcuffed.

"Why, officer, if you wanted a slot for yourself all you had to do was ask the chief to share his . . ."

Suddenly Ray's fist slammed into Carl's face, breaking his nose. Blood poured out of Carl's nostrils as he staggered back against the police car and slid to the ground.

"You son of a bitch. How could you do that to children?" Ray stood over him and gave him a hard kick in the abdomen, then looked at the officer, who bent down to roughly lift Carl back to his feet and shove him into the cruiser. No words came. None were necessary. The reality of what had been going on in that house right in the middle of an average neighborhood was hitting them all. No one had been prepared to deal with something like this. Not in a quiet little town like Parkland.

Innocence had been stolen.

Lives had been broken.

Evil had snuck in and left its vicious mark.

Everyone involved was suddenly and painfully aware of the depths of depravity which could infect a human heart.

Life would never be the same for any of them.

THREE MONTHS
LATER...

Music poured forth from the sanctuary of Parkland Community Church. It was the first weekend of March and signs of spring were just beginning to appear in North Texas. Buds fattened on bare branches; rosebushes greened and sent tall stalks skyward with tiny buds offering the promise of color and scent to greet the warmer weather. Light sweaters replaced heavy winter coats, and spirits in the small Texas town were just a little brighter, warmed by the sun gracing the blue sky.

The church was packed this morning. Very special guests sat near the front, in seats reserved for them in order to accommodate the wheelchair in which Hannah sat.

After six long weeks in the hospital, the first two of which had been spent in the ICU, Hannah had been released to the care of her new foster family, the Garcias, who had taken in her younger sisters since their removal from the Ruiz home. The Garcias were fully devoted to helping Hannah, Leslie, Jessie, and Rosie receive the medical, emotional, and spiritual support they needed to cope with the trauma they had endured throughout their entire lives and, hopefully, learn how to trust again. It would be a lifelong process, but having raised their three children to adulthood and lamenting their empty nest, they were more than ready to give the girls the love and safety they so desperately needed.

Next to Hannah's wheelchair were her three sisters. True, it turned out they were not her biological sisters, as the neighbors had assumed, but their bond was one borne of common survival of some of the worst imaginable abuse. They would be inseparable and key to one another's healing as the years went by.

On the other side of Mr. and Mrs. Garcia sat Mr. Woodruff and his wife. The principal's left arm was in a sling, still recovering from his most recent surgery to repair the damage inflicted by the gunshot wound. His wife looked up at him as the music played, thankful to have him by her side and so very proud of her husband for risking his life to save those girls.

Behind the Woodruffs sat Wendy Miller and her family. Tears of gratitude streamed down Wendy's face as the worship pastor called the congregation to stand. Wendy tried to sing through the lump in her throat without success, so she took a deep breath and listened to the music surrounding her: voices of the rescued children singing "Victory in Jesus" and bouncing along, bursting with giggles, to the beat; Mr. Woodruff's good arm raised in praise to a God who had proven himself very real and incredibly present throughout his recovery.

Carl was behind bars, awaiting trial for his crimes that had been discovered to span six states and involve more than two dozen girls and women over the course of twenty years. Lucya, who, as a young woman, had emigrated to the United States as part of an elite prostitution ring had spent the past twenty years with Carl as a handler of young women and girls like Miranda, Hannah, and the others. After Miranda led the police to her house, Lucya was deported to the Soviet Union where she was fined 100 Rubles then continued working in the human trafficking industry within her home country.

Miranda had been released to an inpatient therapeutic counseling facility after the details of her own victimization had been disclosed and she fully cooperated with the investigation, shedding a bright and disturbing light on what had been going on in the Ruiz home in multiple cities and towns around the country. Miranda would, at last, find true freedom through a relationship with Jesus Christ after being introduced to him by none other than Wendy Miller.

The chief was found, dead, a few hours after the girls had been rescued from Carl's possession. He had driven his police car out to a remote country road and shot himself in the head. The note he had scrawled in the moments before he pulled the trigger revealed the torment of his dark soul, the level of depravity he had reached, the addiction to pornography that had led to pedophilia, and the sick pleasures from which he could no longer find hope of escape.

Violet, Pete, and Nora were able to rent a small house together just three blocks from where their trailers had once stood. This one, though, had a firm foundation. Nora was offered a job as a waitress at the local café and, with her work ethic, soon became a manager and brought home a steady paycheck for the first time in her life. Her oldest boys were still a mess, but her younger children responded to their newfound stability and now-joyful mother with (mostly) obedience and love. Kelley was a huge help to her mother and never ceased to be amazed at the change in their lives after Nora became a Christian. The boys, despite many bumps along the way, would come around eventually. Nora's persistent prayers, along with those of Violet and Pete, would aid that process along.

Hannah, Kelley, and Melody's friendship reached a new level in the weeks following the storm. When Kelley was told what had been going on behind the scenes with Hannah and her sisters, she was shocked and devastated. She and Melody were at

Hannah's bedside in the hospital as much as the nurses would allow, playing music, reading to her, reassuring her that they would not leave her. Despite their disgust at what had been done to their friend, they faithfully came alongside Hannah and loved her through her recovery from her physical wounds.

Hannah would never bear children. The damage done by the botched abortion resulted in her losing her uterus in order to save her life. Though she would grieve this fact for many years, she would eventually see that not even this terrible complication would be wasted by a merciful God who had plans to use even her deepest pain for good.

Dr. Sanderson was arrested and would spend time in prison for his involvement in the trafficking ring, along with several other professionals, local government authorities, and upper-level state officials who had been frequenting the brothel. The entire city was reeling in shock as name after name was broadcast on the local news. So many secrets. So many double lives.

As the final line of the last hymn was sung, the pastor stepped to the podium and addressed the congregation.

"Friends, I want to recognize some very special people who are here today. What a blessing to look out and see the Woodruffs and Garcias here in the front! We have been praying for you all over the past months." He looked at Hannah, smiling. "And you, sweet Hannah, are a miracle. We cannot tell you how thankful we are to see you looking so strong and healthy. We know you have a long road of recovery still ahead, but you are part of our family now, and we are here for you. All of us. Just look around, friends." He motioned with both arms stretched wide. "Do you realize what we have here in this room? This is the Kingdom of God at its finest! You, brothers and sisters, are the hands and feet of Jesus, and I am very, very proud to stand before you as pastor. Well done.

"But the fight is far from over. Our church is entering into a partnership with Mrs. Wendy Miller and her organization to put an end to the trafficking industry in North Texas. We need you. We need volunteers and donors to help keep the wheels turning so we can identify and rescue every girl and boy who is trapped in slavery. It is a huge task but one to which I believe God has called us. Pray that He will show you what role He has given you in this fight, then do whatever He tells you to do.

"Girls . . ." The pastor stopped and looked at Hannah, Leslie, Jessie, and Rosie each in turn. "We love you all. You are not alone."

Hannah looked at her sisters, tears trickling down her cheeks, and smiled. Mr. Garcia saw her and reached across the three younger girls to take her hand, giving it a fatherly squeeze before letting go. The congregation broke into applause and the pianist began to play again, a joyful and upbeat song of celebration. A song of hope that everyone sang—together.

THE END

TWENTY FIVE
YEARS LATER...

In the quiet of the Children's Protection Center, a little girl stood. The only sound was the ticking of the clock on the wall above the social worker's desk. The child appeared to be about six years old, though small for her age and very thin. The room was filled with stuffed animals of every size, shape, and color: Bears, rabbits, puppies, kittens—all brand new. Four large jars full of colorful beads and sealed with white lids perched atop a small bookcase. A sage-green bowl full of more beads was placed in front of a fifth jar, which was a little more than half full. Plaques were carefully arranged above a desk, along with framed photos of Superman, Batman, Cinderella, and Snow White. The little girl's frightened eyes stayed cast down, though, only occasionally daring to peek up at the kind woman who knelt before her, gently cradling her small hand in her palm.

"This is Miss Rose. Her job is to help little girls like you and me, to make you safe." Hannah stood slowly, allowing the child to decide when to let go of her hand. Miraculously, she did not. She looked at her sister and smiled through tear-filled eyes, trading off the conversation with a nod.

"Look around," said Rose. "It seems to me you could use a friend. One of these animals is yours to keep and take with you. You can choose your favorite when you are ready." Rose smiled at the child, keeping her eyes soft and giving her all the time she needed.

The girl looked up, glancing furtively around the room. Despite herself, her eyes lit up for a split second as they landed on a light brown puppy with long, dark brown ears and big blue eyes. Its red tongue dangled in a friendly pant. A simple pink collar adorned its neck. Hannah stooped once again, close enough to follow the child's line of sight.

"You like the brown puppy?" she asked quietly. The little girl gave one quick nod and looked down once again. Rose took three steps over to the puppy and carefully plucked it from its place on the shelf, cradling it like a baby as she carried it over to the girl. She passed it to Hannah when the child tensed and allowed Hannah to hand it to her. The little girl took the puppy into her arms and buried her face in the soft fur of its back, turning away from the women and allowing herself to look up for a moment and take in her surroundings.

Rose walked over to the jars.

"Do you see these jars full of beads?" The child nodded. Rose continued: "Every single one of these beads represents a little girl or little boy just like you who has come into my room feeling sad. All of these kids were hurt just like you have been. I want you to know that you are safe here. No one is going to hurt you anymore. You are not alone. Would you like to pick a bead? You can pick the one you think is the most like you."

She took the green bowl and brought it over, allowing Hannah to be the go-between once again. The little girl scanned the myriad of colors and shapes, shyly reaching out and moving the top layer aside to see the ones underneath. An iridescent blue leaf-shaped bead emerged and she picked it up, carefully turning it over and over in her tiny hands, scratching at the ridges on the leaf with dirty fingernails. Rose brought over the partially-filled jar and allowed her to drop the bead inside.

"You are not alone," she repeated. "Miss Hannah and I are going to help you, okay? We have a safe place for you to sleep tonight, and we hope you will let us become your friends. You can talk about whatever you want whenever you want. You get to choose. No one is going to hurt you anymore." Rose straightened, placing the jar back on the shelf and taking a notepad off her desk with an address scribbled on the top page.

"This is the foster family who will take her in. I have used them many times—wonderful people. She will do well with them." Rose tore off the sheet of paper and handed it to Hannah. "Once she is settled in, have them call me and we will set up her forensic interview and counseling sessions."

Seeing the fear in the little girl's eyes, Rose stopped. "Don't worry, sweet girl. I promise you are safe now. Miss Hannah and I will be with you as long as you want us to be, okay? We will not leave you alone. We will walk with you through every step and help you as much as you need us to. I know you are so scared. I was just like you, once. But someone rescued me and now, look!" Rose smiled and motioned around her office.

She reached across her desk and picked up an old photograph, a two-by-three inch framed picture of a little girl with blonde curls holding the hand of a police officer. The girl in the photo was not smiling. In fact, she had no expression at all—just an empty, hollow-eyed look of resignation. Rose showed the photo to the child. "This is me when I was two years old. That is the nice man who helped me and took away the bad people who hurt me. Now I get to help you. You're going to be okay. I promise." Rose forced her words through the sudden thickness in her throat, tears betraying her calm. "You are going to be okay." She smiled and the little girl looked up at her, finally meeting her eyes, measuring her expression, weighing her voice.

When the child spoke, her tiny voice broke the silence like pebbles skipping across the calm surface of a puddle. "You wanna hold my puppy too?"

SO, NOW WHAT?

All across the United States, children like Hannah, Leslie, Jessie, and Rose are enduring unspeakable horrors at the hands of child traffickers and their clients. It happens in seedy motels, middle class neighborhoods, and wealthy subdivisions of every major city.

This story was borne out of heartbreak—the realization that a girl I had grown up with back in the eighties was being used our entire childhood and none of us, none of her friends, had any idea what was going on. We just thought she was wild and "loose."

The truth is, she was suffering, as are countless others in our country and throughout the world.

According to rescue1global.org, human trafficking is the second-fastest-growing criminal industry in the world, only trailing the drug industry, with an estimated annual revenue of $42.5 billion. Yes, billion.

Approximately 80 percent of human trafficking is allocated

to forced prostitution.

America is the number one consumer of human trafficking.

According to the Department of Homeland Security, trafficking victims are scattered nationwide in the agricultural, hospitality, restaurant, and domestic work industries, as well as others. They are also found in prostitution that is marketed online, on the streets, and in businesses fronting as legitimate enterprises, such as massage parlors.

These are human beings who have often been promised jobs or the American dream, only to find themselves enslaved and used over and over again until they either die or are rescued.

From 2007–2017 the National Human Trafficking Hotline received reports of 34,700 sex trafficking cases in the United States.

The National Center for Missing and Exploited Children estimated that in 2017, one in seven endangered runaways reported to them were likely sex trafficking victims.

The fact is, sex trafficking is in every community—including yours.

So how do we know? How can we identify trafficking victims today?

Here are some warning signs you need to know, adapted from information provided by the Polaris Project (polarisproject.org) and Innocents at Risk (innocentsatrisk.org):

1. They may appear malnourished.

2. They may show signs of physical abuse, such as bruises or

scars, even broken bones.

3. They avoid eye contact or social interaction, especially with authority figures.

4. They may lack identification documents such as birth certificates or social security cards.

5. They may appear to be poor, lacking personal possessions, living in motels, in their vehicle, or at work.

6. They may be seen checking into hotels with older men.

7. They may have a tattoo (or brand) marking them as property.

8. They often have untreated sexually transmitted diseases.

9. Establishments engaged in sex trafficking have security measures in place, such as barred windows and thick curtains that are always closed.

10. Victims are often not allowed to go into public alone or allowed to speak for themselves.

If you are victim of human trafficking you need to understand three very important things:

1. *You are not alone.* What you are going through, unfortunately, is happening to millions of others just like you. Know that rescues happen every single day.

2. *There is hope.* There are people in every community, people in authority and even your neighbors or teachers, who will help you! They will teach you job skills, lead you to counselors who will walk with you as you start a new life, and cheer you on as you make good decisions and succeed.

3. *You are loved.* Yes, the story you just read is fictional, but the facts Wendy Miller presented to Nora Collins are not. There is a very real God who sent His son, Jesus, to die on a cross and pay the price for your sins. He then rose from the dead three days later. This is true. God has everything in place for you and longs for you to accept his free gift of salvation, surrendering control of your life to him. He is kind and he is loving. He will make you into the person you were created to be and lead you into a new way of life. You can trust him. He will never leave you and never turn his back on you. He will use the pain you have endured and create beauty from the ashes of your life.

If you need help, or know someone who does, call the National Human Trafficking Hotline at 1-888-373-7888 (TTY: 711) or text 233733.

◆ ◆ ◆

If you would like to know more about Jesus Christ and have someone help you as you begin to follow him, there are *many* wonderful churches in our country that will do that very thing, or just email me at alifeofsimplejoys@gmail.com and I'll assist you in finding someone in your area who can connect with you. I'll also send you a Bible if you don't have one.

Thank you for reading my book.

To God be the glory.

Jeanine Joyner

THANK YOU...

Kyle. For putting up with my revisions of revisions that often got worked out way past our bedtime.

My kids. Always remember who you are and Whose you are. Your mama loves you to the moon and back.

Candy. Your insight is what made this story work. Thank you for sharing your knowledge with me. Let's have tea again soon!

My friends who read the early chapters and gave me honest feedback...you know who you are. I don't dare try to list you all for fear of leaving one out! You are my people. You make me better.

ABOUT THE AUTHOR

Jeanine Joyner is a wife, mom, and avid reader. Having always dreamed of becoming a writer, she ventured from the blog world to creating her first novel, which you now hold in your hands!

You can read more of Jeanine's writing on her blog, alifeofsimplejoys.com.

She is also on Instagram at @alifeofsimplejoys, on Facebook at A Life of Simple Joys, and on Twitter at @lifesimplyjoy.

Her hope is that this book will open the eyes of the reader to the realities of sex trafficking and spur them to action, and especially that this story will fall into the hands of victims who desperately need rescuing.

You are not alone.

Made in the USA
Coppell, TX
06 December 2020

43232715R00095